FRIENDS AND DARK SHAPES

Kavita Bedford

FRIENDS AND DARK SHAPES

Europa
editions

Europa Editions
1 Penn Plaza, Suite 6282
New York, N.Y. 10019
www.europaeditions.com
info@europaeditions.com

Library of Congress Cataloging in Publication Data is available
ISBN 978-1-60945-664-1

Bedford, Kavita
Friends and Dark Shapes

Book design by Emanuele Ragnisco
instagram.com/emanueleragnisco

Cover photo © Andrew Quilty

Prepress by Grafica Punto Print – Rome

Printed in the USA

CONTENTS

For my Father

And did you get what
you wanted from this life, even so?
I did.
And what did you want?
To call myself beloved, to feel myself
beloved on the earth.

"Late Fragment" by Raymond Carver

FRIENDS AND
DARK SHAPES

SPRING

T he year after my father died, I move into a share house. I know Niki from parties in our younger years, and I first met Sami at a friend's garage sale years ago where I wanted a pair of dice cufflinks, and he laughed at me.

There is a spare room in the house that still needs to be filled. The three of us want a gender balance. So, on a Saturday, we hold housemate interviews.

Here, people gravitate mostly towards friends of friends, because that's how you get anything. But we decide we want to branch out and to try someone new. We put it all over Facebook and online groups and people's bios spill out as desperate pleas. The profiles people make to find a room in cities are an inventory of likes and carefully crafted personal stories, and we quickly become pros at reading between the lines.

The first guy comes at 11 A.M. and has a dad who is a big name in the film industry, and we feel an embarrassed thrill ripple through us when he arrives. He is a 'lad', but a rich lad, who tells us that sometimes he likes to slum it, and he wears all his contradictions in a jarring mix of Adidas button-up pants and Ralph Lauren polo shirts with Ray-Bans, and his gold ring glints as he shakes Sami's hand. We see that he drove to our place in a beat-up BMW that is now parked out front at an awkward angle, creating traffic problems in the narrow street.

He speaks to us in long drawls, which makes him seem unimpressed by everything. He is holding a big takeaway cup and slurping through a straw. And he nods at us, shaking the cup, and in his long drawl he says, banana and berry smoothie, I fucking love the combo.

He runs a bar that we all know in the area that his dad bought for him, and it means long nights, so he wants to live somewhere within walking distance.

Fuck, these house meetings are the worst hey, he says, and we agree out loud.

He tells us he knows the boys who live on the neighbouring street. We know those boys too. They are part of a local hip-hop band, and they have made some songs about different pretty girls in different streets of Sydney, and their songs have started to play on the radio. They party all night and have a slouchy worn leather couch on the porch, and there's always a different group of young girls passed out on that couch, while the boys blare Aussie hip-hop and wave the national flag proudly. And although they are always friendly and wave when we walk by, there is something jangled and uneasy that comes out of that house.

He walks through the space, peering over his sunglasses. We trot behind him and tell him about the electricity and the quarterly bill breakdown, and he lists the rooms in our house, saying, I mean, it's just bedroom, bedroom, kitchen, lounge, bathroom, bedroom. He says, it's not for me, and he walks out slurping the remains of his smoothie.

The second guy arrives at lunchtime and he says he is a sound artist and that he creates poetry based on codes. The patterns binary codes make can be beautiful, he says, and you can create shapes out of these.

He asks if our internet plan includes unlimited data and measures the room to see if it can fit his equipment, and Sami tells him about the wi-fi bundle and asks him, how does computer poetry sound, and the guy says he randomly generates code to match with words and then he performs these in part-binary and part-words. He says it makes him feel like some mad dada guy in Zurich. He has to get going as he needs to prepare for a collective poetry reading and then he looks puzzled and says, but how random is any of this really? I mean, those dada guys cut out bits of paper with words on them, but still they chose the words, and even those words were a product of a time and a place, and sometimes, he says, I wonder how much in life really is sequential randomness as we often like to pretend it is.

The third guy tells us that he has just arrived from California, and this we already know. He likes Foals and The xx and anything dreamy and wanted to move to Australia because it suited his lifestyle but with more sun, sun, sun. This we also know. We know a lot about him before he arrives from his Facebook profile.

He walks around the house talking, repeating his likes and dislikes but telling us his story, and as he speaks he touches everything. The kettle. The benchtop. He even fingers the curtains.

I mean, I'm just interested in good vibes, you know. I want to resonate with everything.

His hair is tied up in a ponytail, and he wears loose cotton clothing and Birkenstocks and has thin woven bracelets along his arm. As he forcefully speaks of good energies, as though willing them into the space, he seems to grow while we three seem to shrink.

There is no room for questions. He tells us things we never asked.

He tells us his brother travelled here once, before he died, and he did a fruit picking season and he always said go to Sydney. Go to Sydney, he'd said, and you will feel free.

So, I think, yeah, maybe in Sydney the ghosts won't follow me so much, you know. I figure you're a country even younger than ours, so the haunting might stop here, right?

I feel a thud of recognition. But there is something about

the way he says all of this, like it is some showman script, so I don't show that I agree.

Everything in most houses is dead, he continues. I have been to so many houses in this city and I feel the occupants and their furniture are dead, you know. He says that music is spiralling downwards and everything feels the same, and he has travelled and done so many things in his life already at thirty, but sometimes he feels so exhausted at the thought that he needs to keep going and that no one is saying anything new. Coachella is dead. Burning Man is dead. I want to feel light, he says. I want to feel I can breathe again. It suffocates me. You have so much sun; why are you people so dead?

He eventually stops and rests against a doorframe and holds his hands wide, framing us all in the picture.

But your kitchen table is alive.

We are all silent for a beat, and Sami looks at me and Niki and takes charge of the conversation, giving long affirmative mmm sounds, but I notice he doesn't offer a beer or something to drink like he did with the others.

That evening a last-minute friend of a friend tells us he is interested and he comes over for a beer. He works in a guitar shop, and he says he thinks Afghan hounds are the best dogs in the world, and we look at pictures of the hounds together, and he laughs easily.

We end up picking a friend of this friend to make our new home in this city.

2.

Chairman Mao lives next door to us, in the subsidised housing commission flats, and his room looks right down into our backyard. It's the perfect distance to throw things. Which he does, often.

In the beginning we could understand the irritation caused by a group of young people having parties. But rather than yell or complain he expressed his frustration via objects that would come sailing out of his window and land in the backyard. At first it was just pieces of trash. But he realised the power he wielded when during one party he threw a glass bottle and it smashed on the brick courtyard. A girl's arm was cut and another guy received a small gash in his forehead. People started screaming.

Another bottle was hurled from the window and everyone ran inside. The cultural revolution has begun, Sami muttered.

From then on he knew how to control the crowds and activities at our house.

We have never seen his face. But everyone seems to agree that he is a small Asian man with a long wispy beard who sometimes rummages in the dumpsters in the back alley. He is an elusive character. When police were called we could hear them banging on his door, but as far as we could tell, he never answered.

Lately the bottle smashing has increased. And the triggers are becoming more strange and inexplicable. Just this morning we were all drinking tea, reading the paper and doing the weekend quiz together outside when a beer bottle shattered next to us.

And it seems it is happening to houses all along the street. His apartment has prime viewing position over the shorter terrace houses, like some panopticon on the back streets of Redfern. This week, a note was pushed under our door calling for neighbourly resistance and urging us to alert the police whenever it happened to 'raise our united voice against his actions' and to 'mount our solidarity.'

The note comes from one of the houses that has recently been sold to a young lawyer couple, and all of us feel uneasy about this note. Without much discussion of its implications, we stick it to our fridge.

As kids, we weren't allowed to go to the street we are now living on. Parents rerouted their cars past the inner-city shortcut with a wag of the finger and a long 'tsk' directed down its narrow frame. It is part of The Block in Redfern, a concrete plot provided to the Aboriginal people thirty years ago that became known as rough 'housing' land. This street is a government-commissioned space next to train tracks and broken telegraph poles and squashed terraces. A space forced to be reimagined into a spiritual reckoning. A block of land filled with different tribes and families ripped from their waterways, and the salt air, and their songs.

Real-estate advertisements have started calling our street an 'ideal location', and it is walking distance to the pop-up bars and the growers' markets and the bike-store-cafe. There is a community herb garden and film festivals screen in the laneways.

Two streets away is a telegraph pole with 'Fuck Gentrification' scribbled over it. Just this week, Indigenous protesters have set up camp outside the train station to speak out against the forced housing relocation of local tenants to make way for new developments.

We decide, mainly due to the bottle smashing, to cover the courtyard in astroturf. So, on the first warm day of spring, we buy supplies at Bunnings and prepare for a backyard blitz.

We throw ourselves into the fun and what began as a practical solution now has us daydreaming about purchasing flamingo statues, and wicker chairs, and turning the backyard into some kitsch Florida cabana. We have bought small palms and are in the process of repotting them.

Our new housemate's pretty, delicate features, coupled with his intense hoarding of blue junk, has earned him the nickname Bowerbird. He is distracted because he has a date with a girl he really likes who works at the local cafe, and she is due to arrive at any moment. So, while we are on our knees cutting up the turf and digging our hands deep into the potting mix, he hovers uselessly, not wanting to fully commit to the task at hand and destroy his smart-casual outfit, instead checking his phone every couple of minutes.

The girl arrives and she is a tumble of hair. She pushes her bike, laughing, into the backyard. We all do our hellos and Bowerbird explains the note on the fridge, and Chairman Mao, and the astroturf, and as we work and chat, she sits on our back step and rolls a cigarette and seems in no rush to leave.

She lives on the other side of the suburb, across the park, near a different set of housing commission flats. She lives with one other girl. One night when she was home alone she saw the shape of a man at her front door and could hear him breathing. She freaked out. But in her gut, she knew this man wanted her fear, which made her angry, so she ran to the kitchen and grabbed two saucepans and ran back to the corridor and screamed, fuck off you fucking perv, and began smashing the pans together and just kept up her aggression chant until she saw his shape leave. She is laughing as she says this, and I can feel us as a group become a little bit impressed by the cafe girl.

A lot of the houses on her street are occupied by young

women living together and each one is experiencing something similar. She tells us the police came around later that week and spoke to her. They told her they were taking it very seriously. Several women had complained. The man did the same thing at each house, just watched and breathed heavily, and so far, no physical assaults had been reported. He was probably from the area and knew they were all young women, and one night the police chased him, but he disappeared and there was nothing to charge him with yet. They said, please tell us if you see any-one in the area who is tall, dark and wears a hoodie, and report it immediately. But, she says, she had suddenly shrunk back from the implications of those words.

She says, it's the area, you know. All these layers of different people. The Indigenous community, the housing-commission folk, the students, the young professionals. We move here because we love these contradictions, but sometimes they feel too much, you know? It's almost like everyone feels robbed of their freedom in some way, and so everyone wants to find who took it.

Bowerbird makes a motion for them to go and she stubs out her cigarette and says it was nice to meet us all, and then they walk out the garage door.

We go back to our cabana lounges and silently drink our green tea. At some point, Sami walks inside and takes the note off the fridge door and throws it in the bin. We continue tuck-ing the astroturf into all the corners of the courtyard.

3

Katie and I are drinking tea on a sunny afternoon in her rambling backyard. We have laid out cushions and rugs under the trees. We have both had big nights out, at separate parties, and it is taking all our mental concentration to lift the pot of steaming tea and pour.

Her night was magic mushrooms, bonfire hallucinations and threesomes. Mine was a party where we dressed up as our favourite *Game of Thrones* character. It is the first party I have been to since my father passed, and for my debut I mostly sat on the steps with a bottle of red wine, picking at the label and playing with my plastic sword, occasionally replying in bad ye-olde English and confused wall metaphors when someone spoke to me.

Everything Katie does is wild. She has lived all over the world, in Istanbul, Tehran, Paris, and she has a wild mess of curls and never seems to sleep. She is a couple of years younger than me and told me once that I think about the world of 'tomorrows' too much.

I've always done what I want, and then dealt with the next situation as it arises, she told me matter of factly.

Katie is asking me about the new house and how I like it. She asks me how Aleks, my boyfriend, feels about me moving out with different people. I mean, she says, I know you two haven't exactly been good since . . .

She trails off and I pretend not to notice.

Last night Aleks came over to help me move my wardrobe,

an old bulky thing that didn't fit easily up the narrow stairwell that leads to my bedroom.

Aleks held the wardrobe at the bottom and I tried to steer the tip of it up the stairs, but my hands kept slipping.

You need to move it the other way, he said, and I heard him swear softly.

Sami had come in and asked if we wanted a hand. We gratefully accepted, and it took almost twenty minutes to inch it, with minute precision, into the bedroom. We were all puffing and swearing, but also laughing.

I didn't think we would make it, said Sami. Aleks and Sami high-fived each other. Aleks and I smiled, and for a moment we were light in each other's presence. I offered to buy them both a beer to thank them, but Sami looked at his phone and said he had to go.

Oh, Aleks said, and I noticed he looked disappointed. We both walked up the road to the bar in silence, our arms at our sides.

Sami seems nice, he said, and I agreed.

That wardrobe was a monster, he added.

We sat for a while longer and then he said he had to leave.

Katie's doorbell rings and her friend joins us. She went to the same party as Katie and lies down on the cushions with a sigh of relief. She has aquiline features and an asymmetrical haircut with strands of grey already appearing through the thick brown fringe, and she wears a septum ring and clunky silver jewellery.

She is like an Almodóvar heroine, Katie said before she arrived, and it's true. She talks with her jewelled hands and has long slender fingers. She is beautiful to watch.

We lie back on the rugs and cushions and watch as rainbow lorikeets descend on a date palm and screech away above us.

They come every day at three o'clock, says Katie.

The Almodóvar heroine talks about how she wants to buy a hat. But she is nervous about wearing a hat as she has never worn one before and feels the precedent has not been set.

You are either a hat person or not, she says. And if you are going to suddenly, after years of being a non-hat person, put one on, it must be done with complete confidence.

The birds loosen debris from the tree above and date husks cascade onto us. A branch falls down and hits the friend, who gently says, ouch. The branch is filled with crimson pods half-flowering and Katie laughs and says to her friend, of course only you would get struck by the prettiest branch in the world, while we shake the brown husks and twigs out of our hair.

The doorbell rings again and the partner of the Almodóvar heroine walks in. He nods his head in greeting and lies next to her in the sun. As we continue to talk lazily about the best way to mix a bloody mary, and the pros and cons of living out west, and the ethnic food compared to the city brunch food, and laugh about weird neurotic habits we picked up in our teens like nail-biting and scab-picking, he remains silent. Instead he brushes her hair, and flicks the grass off her legs, and strokes her eyebrows. They lie back in the sun and dissolve into each other.

I feel upset. I can't tell if I am beginning to fall in love with her a little bit, or if I want to be her; maybe they are always the same thing. With women my age, I have a desperate desire to be them; I watch them put on bright red lipstick, laugh on the phone while walking down King Street, distractedly touch a mole on one cheek in a cafe in Surry Hills. I imagine this woman, trying on hats and adjusting the tilt of the brim with her long, ringed fingers, smiling, anchored to her world.

Katie shows us funny videos of sloths on YouTube. My phone rings, and it is a man saying he has a work gig for me, and when I hang up I feel tired from being around all these people, and I quietly grab my bag from the couch and slip out her front door.

4.

To pay the rent, I've begun working as a freelance journalist. I have found another part-time job working for an organisation in the suburbs teaching media skills, which provides me with an office a couple of days a week. And the rest of the time, I wander around the city, hustling for new jobs and pitching stories.

Today I am meeting Paul, a photographer. I contacted him when I saw some work he did about everyday moments of Sydney: specifically, in the city's suburbs, which people don't normally care to take photos of or talk about.

Paul tells me his girlfriend has just found out she's pregnant, and so he needs works that is flexible, but he also wants to take photos of subjects he cares about, which is always a fine balance, he says. He keeps stopping halfway through talking to blow his nose and then apologise. It's the hay fever, he says, this city goes pollen crazy from the wattle in the springtime.

Paul and I are going to meet with a woman who has set up a hijab clothing store in a mall in a suburb out west.

In the car driving to the clothing store, he tells me he spends the rest of his time working as a night stay for people with disabilities. It is back- and heart-breaking work, he says. Some of the people who work as night carers in the disability services are like him, who has a brother with a disability, and so they come at it with so much love. But they feel it all too much because it is at home and at work, and there is often little separation of the self, and often these are the people who leave after a while. Some of the others don't understand so much, and the night shifts pays all right, but they take all the outbursts and bodily problems of the people personally, and to survive they grow an armour, and they roll their eyes and make jokes, and roughly heave the clients about like feeble pieces of flesh. And often it is these people who stay.

He has a favourite client, who often asks him to come in the afternoon rather than at night so he can have company in the sunlight. And they go to a park near the clinic, and there is a little ice-cream shop close by, and it is their ritual to get ice cream and then feed pieces of the waffle cone to the pigeons. This man laughs so much when the birds come that it is infectious, and Paul always leaves feeling lighter and happier. That is the truth of someone's character: how a person makes you feel after you walk away from spending time with them.

When we arrive at the shop, the owner is choosing fabrics from huge swatches, and she grabs my arm in a familiar way and pulls me into her space, saying, which one do you reckon, this one or that one? I point to a slightly deeper magenta than the other and she nods and says, yep, I knew it.

She was born in Syria and moved here when she was twelve, and she tells us she was originally studying to be a lawyer, and then laughs and rolls her eyes at us, typical Arab parents, right. But she says that she struggled to find clothes to wear to her classes.

I had just made the choice to put on the abaya and I was happy about that, she says, even though it was after September 11. But, you know, the thing that bothered me most was I was young and I wanted to look damn hot.

You know, before this, we were getting our clothes from overseas, and they had nothing to do with the fashion here, or else we had to go to the stores out in the suburbs that our mums shopped in. I mean, what young woman wants that? I wanted to be fashionable, and look beautiful, but also honour my faith, you know.

So she started to make her own clothes.

While studying for my law exams, she says, I would have this sewing machine next to me and in breaks I started making my own clothes with nice fabrics, and little features like a cinched waist, or a hot little belt, but still modest, right. And soon some of my friends started asking me to make it for them. And then I realised there was this huge gap in the market in Australia.

She is jokey and easygoing, and also passionate about her fashion and why it is important.

Obviously now it's becoming huge, she continues. Which is so exciting. You have fast-fashion brands like Uniqlo and H&M, and then big designers like Dolce & Gabbana getting on board. But there was nothing like this when I was growing up, and that wasn't very long ago.

She takes us around the shop, and while Paul trails behind us taking photos, she speaks to me about different cuts and lengths, and we swap our likes and dislikes in current fashion, and she tells me what shades would work best against my skin colour.

I admire her eyebrows, which are perfectly waxed and shaped, and which frame her face, also made up impeccably. Although there are only a few years between us, I suddenly feel unfeminine and very young with my make-up-free face and cut-off high-waisted jeans and loose T-shirt, an aesthetic that loses its trendiness in just a twenty-minute drive out of the city. Instead it looks glum against the spangles and popping colors, like I didn't have the imagination to get dressed properly. My mother often tries to coerce me into Indian reds and sparkles and embroidered skirts, and is exasperated by the ill-fitting jumpers and second-hand jeans that my friends and I revel in, and here, with this sparkling woman, I can finally understand it.

She shows me her Instagram account and says it is funny but also sometimes disturbing that she still gets the occasional message telling her what she is doing is haram. She says it's only ever men who feel the need to point this out. She says there are so many people in her community who say that women enjoying their beauty defies Allah. She says she thinks they are scared of what beauty makes them feel. These people don't belong to any form of Islam I am interested in, she says. To keep faith, you also have to find a way that makes sense for you in the modern day.

When we get back in the car, Paul sneezes again, and curses, and then says, how do you feel, and we both agree that when we left her we felt giggly. That, he says, starting the car, that's the character you write, then.

The next morning, I pitch it to a newspaper. A week later I hear back from the editor who says that while he likes the modest fashion movement, it needs reworking to focus on the refugee angle. He says before the piece can run, I need to make it more about Syria, and the conflict, and her pain, and to please turn it in by the end of the day.

5.

I go to a small place out in the western suburbs, near the office where I work part-time, that is at the back of a family-run Chinese herb store. Inside it's all textures and bitter smells: cellophane packets filled with tisanes, crunchy dried barks crammed into baskets, and twisted roots hanging from the ceiling with pieces of twine that remind me of those squealing baby mandrake myths. We are treating my gut, which has been throbbing and squirming like some ferret inside me for the past year.

The old man offers massage services; the hard, dry kind that pinch the skin and force a cry, but also make you certain that pain is the only way to get to the root of problem. His daughter offers acupuncture services and they work side by side.

Most of my friends would roll their eyes at the thought of working with their parents because they'd feel they weren't making their mark. I think how splendid it must feel to be part of a family trade. And the two of them together are kind; the type of kind that allows you to just be silent. This is a rare gift. I always feel close to tears when I see them.

The daughter takes me to the back of the shop to a tiny room with two little beds set up and a makeshift curtain to go around each. It is a bit like a change room at a market stall, just a loose curtain blowing in the wind.

She gently adjusts the pillow. She is serene and graceful, and her skin always has a clear sheen to it, which makes her glow, and when I ask her how, she says she does vipassana, the silent meditation, every year. She says, it's important to create a time to be silent every year; there's a lot of noise in the world.

I lie on my back and she places a hot box stuffed with herbs on my stomach so the steam will go into my belly to ease some of the pain. She twitches the curtains briskly and leaves.

I hear her ushering a woman into the neighbouring change room, and this other woman talks so loudly through the thin curtain separating us that I can hear her trying to heave herself, huffing, onto the little bed.

She tells the acupuncturist she is shvitzing like a heifer. She says her thighs are sweating like a newborn calf. She says her bikini waxer has recently gone on holidays, and she is growing a thicket down there, and she says, it has never been the same since childbirth anyway, and how about that heat. It sounds like some kind of crazed monologue.

The acupuncturist comes back to me and picks up the herb box and turns me onto my belly and taps the fine points of needles into different parts of my back, and says things like meridian, and chambers, and flow, and chi, and organised principles, and I start to get drowsy and then she pulls the curtains and leaves me to my dreamy state.

While I lie silently with needles in my back the woman next door keeps talking. I try to picture the acupuncturist's face as she listens to the growing list of this woman's bodily exclamations. Oh, my back, she says, my neck, my pussy, and my . . . And she bursts out laughing, and her laughter seems to shake the little store with its tied bundles of herb that could blow away any minute in the wind. Then I hear the pull of the curtain as the acupuncturist walks out, and we are both left in the rippling silence.

When it is time to leave I pull on my clothes. I am told to go out to the front of the store and that the acupuncturist will come out for payment in a moment. As I sit waiting I look at the mounds of goji berries, and lapsang souchong, and fermented root, and the father twitches his mouth in the gesture of a smile, and I shyly smile back. The acupuncturist comes outside and hands me a bottle of dark pills, and tells me the times to take them and the amount to take, and then she touches my arm gently and says to me, you are holding on to things too tightly and too deeply. It is making your aura muddy. I pay quickly and leave the little house made of herbs.

6

We are chopping up vegetables at our share house for dinner on a Sunday night in our attempt to replicate some idea of a traditional family.

Have you noticed how everyone our age says they are so busy, Niki says, but like a hashtag humblebrag, like it's something to be proud of?

It's as if by working two jobs, she says, and setting up social-justice fundraisers, and holding a pop-up eatery dinner, and exhibiting at the latest warehouse gallery, and drinking the newest rosemary-infused gin, and posting it to Instagram with the right hashtags, and then making it to yoga and BodyAttack classes the next morning, we are proving our worth.

We are standing side by side at the kitchen bench and Niki is dicing garlic and shallots, occasionally wielding the knife in the air when she says something, and I move my chopping board away from her slightly.

Niki just lost one of her side jobs and has been stressing about money all week. She is earning what is technically below the minimum wage working in graphics at a fashion magazine and so she takes other contracts to make ends meet.

She was picked out as a model when she was sixteen, and it was her ticket out of the small backwards coastal town in South Australia where hers was the only Asian, let alone Cambodian, family.

My dad escaped the Khmer Rouge, she says, and he was so

silent growing up and I never understood why; all I knew was, when I grew up, I wanted to be around noise.

She spent dizzying months between apartments in London and Tokyo and Milan crammed with young girls from all over the world, who all started to look the same with their small bodies and huge heads, living on air for their dreams, and a meanness began to settle into their starved bones.

So many of us stopped bleeding, she says, we floated so far away from any idea of natural. I used to dream about waves and the ocean and the feel of wattle against my skin. And when I finally found the strength to get out, almost a decade later, I left that world of glamour with nothing to show for it and had to start again here.

I wanted to grow up so fast so I ran away only to have to come running back to my parents. I mean, she says, taking a breath and correcting herself, not everyone has parents that can even support them to do that. I'm one of the lucky ones.

Niki is always 'putting things in perspective.' When she is upset or angry or hurt and begins to tell us about it, she will stop herself midway and shake her head as though she has been caught out yet again by her indulgence. Niki doesn't correct others, only herself, so the effect can be like a yoyo of her thoughts. I sometimes wonder what she would discover if she let the thought run its course.

We have a mutual friend who also 'puts things in perspective', but she does it to others, like when a friend was upset about being fired, she said, well, at least you had a job to be fired from, not like in Yemen. And when another friend spent about an hour rehashing her recent break-up at a bar, she said, I'm sorry, I just can't anymore, it's just that there are people fleeing Aleppo and this is, well . . . And she stood up and walked out of the bar.

She works in refugee resettlement, and she is frustrated, and her capacity for caring is worn.

Niki throws sesame oil, onion, carrots, and garlic into the wok, and there is a sudden eruption of pungent steam. Sami, who has just walked into the kitchen, starts coughing, and I fumble to turn on the kitchen fan.

Sami has been busy in his room preparing legal notes for the start of his week. He yawns loudly and pulls beers out of the fridge, stretching as he says he is a short-burst thinker, and that his optimal work is done in intense four-hour periods. He says he recognises how his brain works and he wants to quit his job in law. But he doesn't know how to tell his parents. He tells us his parents are always proudly posting things in their family WhatsApp chat about his job and his sister who works as a diplomat.

If I leave law, I will be deleted from the chat, he says, half laughing.

His parents came from Palestine, and he says they just won't understand. They already don't understand this living situation. Try explaining a 'share house' to Palestinian parents, he says, and how I live with women that I cook with, and share a bathroom with, but who I am not married to.

Do they want you to be married, asks Niki as she grabs the tofu and tamari sauce and the chopped eggplant, broccoli, and red peppers to drop into the wok.

They are upset I haven't found a nice Muslim girl to settle down with.

Niki rolls her eyes and Sami catches her. What?

I always hear you do this spiel about your family when girls are around and they lap it up. You get laid. A lot. You are such a player, she says, laughing.

He turns to me and I have to nod. Women flock to Sami. He looks sheepish.

My friend who is Assyrian, says Niki, has never even had sex and she's our age, because she is a woman and hasn't found someone from her community to marry. It's not a very big community so it's slim pickings, Niki says. And it's so strange, because this woman dresses the sluttiest of anyone I know, and goes to the tackiest bars, so men always think she is up for it too. And I just feel so bad for her, she clearly wants to be sexual, but she feels she has to hold onto it for the backwaters of the Sydney Assyrian scene.

Sami opens the drawers and takes out a stack of knives and forks and spoons and chopsticks, and Niki and I look at him.

What are you doing, she asks.

Setting the table. Everyone has a right to their implement of choice, he says, and he lays them all in a heap in the centre of the table, while I collect bowls and check on the brown rice.

Bowerbird messages us to say he won't be home for our Sunday dinner and to eat without him. He has been spending more and more time at the cafe girl's house.

I also receive a message from Aleks thanking me for the invite, but saying that he is tired and he might stay home tonight.

I am about to put my phone away when Niki points at it and yelps.

Sami turns to look also as they see my mail icon with a red button stating 7700 unread messages.

How, she says. How does that even happen?

It's my shame, I say, throwing the phone back into my bag, and taking away a bowl from the table and returning it to the shelf.

But you work with words and communication stuff, says Niki. You should really tell people before they hire you.

I think how people organise their emails is a sign of something deeper, she says. It's a disorder. You have a cluttered soul.

Well, unread mail could also be a sign of overwhelm, Sami says kindly. Some people have calendars that are colour coordinated and the year is structured and planned in the tight little boxes. I mean, do you want that life?

I am sort of jealous, I say, that they have the kind of life where they have the confidence to plan ahead like that when there is so much uncertainty.

Here, says Niki, it's all your subscriptions, and she takes my phone and opens my inbox and we look at my subscriptions from start-ups and self-proclaimed entrepreneurs telling me I can follow my dreams and be anything.

Niki laughs and hits unsubscribe.

We serve up the rice and the stir-fry, take a beer each and sit around our kitchen table. Niki takes chopsticks, I grab a fork, and Sami takes a spoon and knife, and he raises his eyebrows and says, told you so.

Over dinners my housemates and I often fantasise about a different existence. The countryside, once a place to avoid as a kind of mini-death, has started creeping into young people's visions. People around us are talking about how they want to make an honest living by using their hands, one where they live on the rugged south coast of New South Wales and walk among the driftwood on weekends. Friends have done it. Just upped and left their jobs in the city, bought a run-down place to fix up, and picked up small jobs in the local bakery and bar. They walk around barefoot, know to use angle grinders, and surf each morning, discarding their education.

It's the story we discuss with part disdain and part awe over drinks at the latest pop-up bar. We call them 'hipsters' with a curl of our lips and we question the motivation behind it all as we watch their Instagram followers build. But in some ways, maybe it feels like a better prospect than the renting, and the casual work contracts, and the Tinder one-night stands. My housemates and I want to get on with our lives and build something more lasting. We are turning thirty and things don't look like we imagined they would. We are tired. In conversations everyone uses the word 'space.'

What would your dream be, I ask.

A whole shelf in the fridge, Niki says, laughing. Or to be

able to leave a small mess in the kitchen after a long night and not feel guilty about being a bad housemate, and when I come back in the morning it is still there, exactly as I left it, and it's my mess to own, you know.

Sami takes a sip of his beer and shrugs his shoulders.

Maybe I would like to try living abroad for a while. But I am not sure I really could. My parents have risked so much to come to this country, and they only ask for time with us in return. They wouldn't understand why I would want to leave, and I'm not always sure I do either.

Where would you move if you could, asks Niki. To New York, or to London?

No, he says, those cities just feel like Sydney on crack. It's more people, more opportunity, more speed, and more ambition, says Sami. I don't think I am searching for more, he says. I think I am for searching for different. A different way of living. And to make something that lasts.

Have you seen, Niki says, all these people our age who are armed with succulents at the weekend markets as though they are struggling with the need to nurture and nourish something living. We all pour our love into our share-house pot plants, something that won't be just another short-term promise.

Surely, I say, with all this education, all this opportunity we're told we have, we are meant to burn brighter than this?

Niki picks up a piece of broccoli with her chopsticks and says firmly, these are middle-class problems. I mean, even living like this, we can still buy our coconut water and almond milk, and eat out at Thai restaurants, and go to a music gig here and there and dance.

My dream, Niki says after a while, is to live somewhere small again like I used to when I was little and to draw watercolours of birds, parrots and finches and toucans, a whole menagerie of them. They sort of remind me of all those lost colourful girls I used to live with.

She takes a deep breath, rises and says, it will work out. We are so lucky. She packs up the remains of the stir-fry in a Tupperware container and places it on the communal fridge shelf for one of our lunches tomorrow at work.

7

P aul and I have begun a project. We are doing a series on areas in Sydney that the media describes as being violent, or high in crime, or undesirable. We both spent time in some of these suburbs as children and we know there is more to these places than what the media portrays. So, we decided, we are going to show another perspective, the perspective from the everyday people who make up those communities and the stories they hold.

Today we are meeting in Fairfield, a suburb in which I have spent very little time. We have an angle for the profile of Fairfield, but first, he says, it is important to just walk around and get a feel for the place. The shops, coffee houses, and street benches are filled with groups of older Middle Eastern men, talking and drinking and shouting. The Assyrian shops are stuffed with Orthodox Christian iconography and gold lamé. Iraqi jewellery stores sparkle yellow, bright gold.

As we walk, Paul tells me about how he used to be a graffiti artist. In a different life, he says, laughing. He used to get in trouble with the police a lot, he says, until he met his girlfriend, who helped him out.

It was the same for most kids from around here, he says, some break-ins, some ice, and a bit of just wanting to test the limits. He shows me shining white scars coiling down his neck from when he caught himself on barbed wire running away from the cops.

One of the places where we used to go to hide or to tag or

to just feel some quiet, he says, was underground, and there is a whole sub-group and community there. We would work in train tunnels, stormwater channels, and underground, drains. These guys know what's going on down there better than anyone. Better than the police. It's a weird relationship, where the cops and this crew sort of tolerate each other because sometimes the cops need to ask them about where one of the tunnels leads.

There's a lot of politics involved to be in this crew, he continues. Like, you don't want to let in some guy who is just interested in his own personal glory and who ends up trashing all the tunnels with his tag or giving away all these secret passages, so as a result it can get a bit cultish, as there's initiations and rules and oaths you have to swear.

Paul knows a lot about trains as a result. He tells me that Central Station opened on the site of the old Devonshire Street Cemetery. One time, he says, in the early twentieth century, some soldiers had a brawl and one was shot, and you can still see the bullet marks where it happened.

We walk past a hijab fashion house, 'Beauty Within Da Veil', and past a barber shop filled with young Arab boys getting undercuts.

I tell him something my dad once told me that people used to say, about 'getting off at Redfern', which apparently meant alternative contraception, because it's the last stop before the main destination of the city, and he laughs, and I feel pleased with my one piece of local knowledge to add to this conversation.

Paul says that what really gets him frothing is the idea that all these other people are carrying on with their days above, going to work, fighting with partners, making love, with no idea that there are people moving below them in the underground tunnels and secret chambers of this city. I mean, he says, I can walk the entire distance from Revesby to the city centre underground and no one would even know I was there.

Below the surface of the cracked pavements, he tells me, it is dank and tight, but sort of magic.

He says it feels like where the ghosts of the city truly lie.

But that was all a long time ago, Paul says. Now I don't go down as much as I used to. He says he is a different person, and things change, and now with the baby on the way there is increasingly less time to look at things below the surface.

We loop back towards the train station and past a group of Iraqi men who sit playing checkers in a small square.

When I get on the train to head home, a heavy-set Islander woman sits down beside me, her phone speakers blasting Bitch, get up, get up. She is wearing blue terry-towel shorts and a T-shirt of the South Sydney Rabbitohs, as well as fake Louis Vuitton silver sunglasses and frosted purple lipstick. Her wet hair is bound up in a plastic clasp and she has thick twisted silver hoops in her ears. She nods her head and stares defiantly at me and at fellow commuters as if daring us to tell her to turn down her music.

The train slows down as we approach Redfern and we both get up and wait for the doors to open. A drunk old Vietnamese man stares at my cleavage and lurches towards me. His breath reeks of spirits. She pushes her sunglasses down her nose. Prick, she says, and I watch her in awe as she sashays off the train with her speakers cranking ridin' around in my hood, I got it, I got it.

8.

My friend Andy is riding his bike; his hands are floating up off the handlebars and into the air. He says one day he will be famous for his bike dances. He bought a GoPro to show off his midnight rides. He rides all over the city, headphones plugged in, trance beats thumping wildly, and he lifts himself off his seat, his hands moving like birds migrating in the wind. He wants a YouTube channel.

He pulls up on his bike outside the warehouse party as Caribou beats spill out of the doors.

I am sitting outside in the gutter with a bunch of people who are smoking hand-rolled cigarettes and talking about a different warehouse they went to, in a different suburb, on a different day, and how this one is the same. Andy is gurning. He picks up mid-sentence, completing a conversation he was having with himself.

My girlfriend is always getting fired up about something and I want to care as much as she does. But sometimes when she's talking it scares me how much things matter to her. Like I'm going to be left behind somewhere. Because we can do anything, this generation. We're educated, we live in this fucking amazing city, and we have the possibility and can do anything like never before. But what do you do with that? So many of us are floating or saving up for some day when it will get better. I think it would be better to spend all the money I make doing things I actually love instead of saving it all for some other day. Just a lot of the time, I think I don't want to

live as long as we do these days. I don't want to become a
divorced, sick, still-working, grumpy husk of a man like my
dad and still have so long to go in life. And I don't mean sui-
cide or nothing. I'd just rather live now, and live brightly.

He looks tired. Or maybe I look it, because he stops his
monologue for a moment and comes and puts his hand around
my face and gives me a hug.

There's this other club, he says. In this exclusive club are
those who know what it feels to lose someone forever, and
those that don't. Eventually everyone joins this club. But some
just gain membership a little earlier, he says, still hugging me.

I have known him since we were in high school. Andy lost
his mother at twenty-one, and I know it is still a big part of why
he chases drugs and midnight bike rides and rushes. And in
moments like these, scatty Andy can become the wisest, most
comforting person I know.

Sometimes, you know, Andy says to me, it can be harder to
spend time with those that are not in this club, because it's
exhausting talking about everything in the world except the
biggest thing that is happening to you.

It's true, friends haven't known what to do. I can see them go
limp in the face of it all, and I feel sorry for them, and that they,
that none of us, are equipped with what to do in the face of so
much loss. People don't know how to say it aloud. So they ask if
I want a beer. Or they don't ask, because it rattles them to their
core. Or they talk about it among themselves, where it is safer,
surrounded by others who do not know what it means to lose,
and so they can build a wall between this world and the next.

Are you depressed? Out of all the things they ask, I find this
the strangest and hardest to answer.

Friends had been urging me to go out. But crouching in this
gutter, or standing in the middle of a warehouse dance floor as
Rihanna mash-ups play and beer sloshes, doesn't feel like a real
distraction.

A new ring of strangers has come outside and assembles around us.

Andy rolls a cigarette.

I think I struggle to be a man, he says. Everywhere I go, someone or something is trying to arouse me, trying to get my hormones worked up and get me going, you know, pump all my arousal with advertising and Instagram and drugs and alcohol, and even the fucking news is all clickbait porn now. I feel like I'm walking around like some lab-tested rat, all jacked-up and frothing at the bit. And then I'm told not to act on any of these feelings because they are wrong, wrong, wrong.

I wake up each morning, he says, and it's feminism, and porn, and one-night stands, and Tinder, and rape culture, and politicians who hate abortions, and my girlfriend who had one and said it felt like a vacuum cleaner inside her, and, shit, man, I feel dizzy, and I don't know how I'm supposed to act anymore, you know. I feel like a schizo. I love hanging with the boys at Jubilee Park, and popping pills, and half my friends are girls, and we all get high together, and that one night my friend asked for my help, because she trusted me, so I hugged her, and we were both drunk and I touched her hair, and it turned into more, and she sort of said no, but she also kept going, and then afterwards when she cried, I wondered if I was wrong. But I have to shake away these thoughts or I will go insane . . .

He stops and looks around him, his eyes bugging out, and he shimmies his head and tries to laugh.

That's why I ride my bike. To keep moving in a clear direction, he says to the new group and to no one in particular.

And anyway, one day I will be famous and none of this will matter.

9.

A bar opened mid-week, and it is trendy. Everyone is wearing shirts that are hanging out, and jumpers tied around their waists like they didn't give a fuck when they got dressed this morning, except for the fact that their young lithe bodies defy logic, so they can make even a sack look sexy. On the front page of the menu is a man eating from a bunch of grapes dangling in front of a woman's pussy, and a girl I just met is telling me about the first time she went back home, her other home in Africa, and that rent is so high, so crazy, in Mogadishu. She and I have both been asked as freelancers to write opinion pieces for a major newspaper.

I was there with my uncle, she says, and he was like, that place there, pointing to a medium-sized place, is one million dollars, and I was like, but it's Moga-fucking-dishu.

A girl sitting at the booth in front of us turns around and gives us an agitated look. There's a guy on a makeshift stage who must be her boyfriend the way she is all googly-eyed staring, while he is clearly singing about having sex with some other girl with polka-dot socks and quirky bangs, and I wonder if that makes her feel weird.

But you know, it's people like us that are causing the problem by buying up over there.

I'm not sure what she is talking about.

The diaspora, she says. We went away because of so much injustice and now we're slowly coming back and all these places we can afford to buy others can't so we're creating a whole new class of elite.

The newspaper asked us to write about what it's like being brown and a woman, and how we have handled racism. They didn't put it like that. They said, mysteriously, to write about our experiences 'growing up' in Australia. But we know what they mean.

We haven't decided whether to do the pieces or not, and so we have met up for the first time to talk it through together.

She asks me about how I feel when I go back to India but I say, it's different. I wasn't born there or anything, and people there hardly recognise me as Indian, they think I'm a Spanish tourist. It's all built-up and kinda crazy with its overpasses and its rush and pollution that feels like all the things I reject here have tumbled into a city there.

I tell her my mother is there now. At the beginning of the year, my mother went back to India. She said she needs to be on familiar soil to process what she has lost.

For my mother, coming to this country, everything was new, and like many migrants, she compares her past with this place. Your country, she would say to my father and me, when she was upset by something that happened here and wanted to distance herself.

She calls me often now from Chennai. Sometimes she tells me about what a relative is doing and the food she is eating. I find it soothing to hear her list food and ingredients: dosas, idlis, green coconut chutney, samba, okra. And which auntie makes the best garam masala, and how the fruit vendor comes to the house each week. She also tells me how the kattarikkāy there are so different, sweeter than the ones in Australia. I try not to hear the reproach in her voice.

The thing I'm most scared to talk publicly about in this country is race, this girl admits. I would rather talk about being a sex worker, or about casual sex, or what is it like to have vaginal discharge, all Lena Dunham–style, but race? Fuck no.

Why have they even asked us? I ask, and we laugh, agreeing that neither of us fit into the 'hot' race categories people want to talk about at the moment.

Right now, it's all about the Arab Muslims. And it's super important, she says. But it's like the only viewpoint people want to see. I'm a black Muslim, and at the moment people don't want to hear about that, they're not ready to hear about it. You're half-Indian, half-Anglo, no one has time for that unless it's a some cute Buzzfeed piece about being ethnically ambiguous and being hit on by everyone. It's like they always choose one race to focus on when they feel swamped by Asians or Arabs, and for that moment in time everyone else disappears.

Or, the flip side, she says, where race is the only thing the media want us to talk about. I mean, how often do you see a Syrian face talking about Australian state politics? Or a Somalian allowed to talk about something other than their refugee experience, like the stock market? The fact that we can't have a voice and contribute in everyday current affairs bothers me. Why can't there be someone that looks like you or me on *Neighbours*? Can you imagine a burkini episode on *Home and Away*?

The girlfriend of the singer claps forcefully when he finishes and is glaring at the whole bar now.

Or, she continues, they say talk about your experience, but then make sure it's categorised as an opinion piece, so people really know that it has no factual bearing, and it is immediately minimised and has quotation marks around everything and a picture of you smiling like an idiot in the by-line.

I guess this is our assignment, I respond: write in a colourful way about our background, but at the same time, don't intimidate a Western audience with foreign specifics, or confuse them with details that don't fit into their image of who we should be.

Yeah, she says. Talk universal trauma, post-colonial dreams, mango eyes, coconut-oiled hair, without ever being specific, like Instagram poets, and hey, instant fame. We laugh.

Often there is no vocabulary to even begin to discuss the language of race in this country, she adds. At least in the States they are so hyper-aware of colour, and race, and maybe it is out of control and politically correct, but at least you are allowed to say it aloud and it's recognised. Here, we never seem to be able to say much out loud. His issues aside, Junot Diaz says that in the Dominican Republic they have five different words for different shades of brown, and he says this is important when talking about privilege, because it means there can't be any amnesia about it. Imagine that.

I admire this woman. She is gutsy and she can articulate everything that my mind coils around. But in the past year, I have found my anger about things I once found important diminishing. I find her sense of incredulity and injustice about these things now exhausting. She is right. I don't really think I have any experiences to discuss. Or, rather, it feels like everyone is screaming at each other these days, so certain of their position, and I am not sure that what we need is another opinion.

The last thing we ever want is to come across as ungrateful, she says. Because fuck knows we have it so good. We are safe. We are educated. We have family. We have freedoms beyond so much of the world. And maybe beyond where we came from. But here, in this country, that just becomes another reason we are not allowed to discuss our observations on race and dynamics. Or we cannot talk about how it happens every single day, like a small blunt instrument drumming away, until it becomes a familiar beat that no longer bothers people.

The singer is packing up his equipment. I look at the wall

with a picture of naked women crushing grapes in wooden vats, and next to her is a giant knitted phallus. I hope this woman writes her piece because I won't. I envy her rage and her energy. I just feel drunk from the red wine, and tired, and I wonder if I too am just becoming part of the familiar beat.

10.

The days are growing warmer, and my housemates and I have started to go to art exhibition openings for the free wine. We can slip into the creative scene with ease. We can say things like pastiche, and overlay, and depth of perspective, and know how to pivot quickly and ask other people how the art made them feel. So, no one bats an eyelid when one evening we walk past a small building bright with lights and festive chatter, and then enter, swiping glasses of house red and white as we float into the room.

We all like art well enough. Niki paints, Bowerbird plays guitar, I write sometimes, and, as Sami says, he keeps us afloat because he pays for culture. Most of the people here are only about a decade older than us, and in so many ways this could be us in a few years. We recognise a few people: a sartorial blogger and a semi-famous art reviewer from a newspaper. And there is a buzz being in a room with these successful people. But we still see ourselves as separate.

They are posers, says Bowerbird. And Niki reaches across and flicks his Butter Goods cap and laughs, saying, what, and you aren't?

Fair, says Bowerbird, but you know what I mean. Nothing about this world inspires me to be an artist. These are just rich people. Who happen to make art. That's why we come to take their wine—I'm a modern-day Robin Hood, and he grabs another glass from the table.

Are we also the poor in your scenario, asks Sami, also taking a glass, because that's a fucked-up class view you have there.

The room is filling with people, and we can hardly see what exhibition is showing, and so we fall into the mode of mingling while standing still. Niki grabs ones of the pamphlets lying around and says, great font. We open it and we learn the artist is a woman with Slovakian origins, who feels that lines are the only true form of pure expression left, that everything else is corrupted, and even a line, she poses, what does that mean in a world that is always looking to cast things below and above them.

Heavy, mutters Bowerbird.

A real rush, we hear from a man next to us with a fedora and thick black glasses wearing a vest over a brushed white cotton shirt with artfully rolled sleeves. He is talking at a small blonde woman who is patiently listening to his impressions of the artist. Bowerbird snorts and whispers, he is just telling her what's in the pamphlet, and then he adds, I don't even think his glasses have real lenses in them.

We often become mean at these things. We grab more wine.

Pfftt, says Bowerbird, so this woman draws lines about hierarchy so it can hang on the wall of some socialite?

Niki laughs. I think Bowerbird has just figured out the art industry.

It's people like this that give art a whole elitist construct, says Bowerbird, sweeping his hands to take everyone in. Like, a real artist is someone who is practising their craft daily, and it's a humble and gratifying way to live, you know. But then you have these people, where it is just launches, and daddy's money supporting them to pursue their dreams. And it sounds good to say you are creative, and so they get the kudos, without ever knowing struggle, which really is the key part that teaches anyone any kind of self-discipline.

Um. Projection much, says Niki. Are you jealous of their money?

Miserably so, says Bowerbird, and he laughs.

You do realise we're entitled also, says Sami, and he leans across to the table and passes us each more wine.

Not like this, says Bowerbird.

But you have decided to lead this life and pursue your music. Whatever the end game is, you're impoverished out of choice, not necessity, Robin Hood.

We need to remember we are very lucky, says Niki, nodding furiously.

Also, Sami continues, I hate to break it to you, but a lot of the best art and literature came from some pretty privileged folk. We would never have access to some of the greatest work if they didn't have the wealth to make it happen. Anyway, we don't even know these people are all rich. They could just be aspirational like us.

Well, they all look it and speak like it, says Bowerbird. God, I hate posh Australian accents so much. I mean, is that even a thing our country can pull off?

We laugh and start saying long twanging drawls of daaaaarling to each other and drink more wine.

A couple drifts over to us, leaning in to hear what we are talking about. She is wearing a sequined kaftan, her hair a perfect balayage, and he is much older with a chiselled jaw and asks us what we are discussing.

I say social capital, because it is something I once learned at university, and it sounds right, and I know it will piss off Sami and he throws me a glance. These attractive people nod their heads, click their tongues, and say, mmm. They eventually wander off. We make some more judgmental comments about the kaftan lady, while I secretly wonder how I can get my hair to look like hers.

Niki grabs another wine and her mouth sets into a tight red-stained O.

When we finally make it to the fringes of the room we see the walls are painted white and three paintings hang in a row.

There are lines. Lines going up, lines going down, lines across and zigzagging—it almost makes me dizzy. In one painting they are different shades of red. In another they are black and grey, and the final painting is done in the negative, so the canvas is black with pale white lines.

There is a beat. None of us know whether to scoff or if it is actually good.

I feel something between confused and nothing, says Niki. It feels like people keep prodding me to have important reactions to things, but more and more I just feel empty. She looks like she is about to cry, and she lets out a baleful hiccup.

I don't even know what I'm working towards anymore, she continues. Is this the end game? Do we just keep on, heads down, making ourselves so tired to get somewhere like this, a wall that just feels empty? What's the point? And then a small tear actually starts to roll down her cheek, and Sami puts his arm around her and says, all right, home time.

On our way out, Niki grabs two empty wine glasses from the table with the emblem of the gallery on them and stashes them into her bag and hiccups again and says, ours now, and Bowerbird high-fives her.

11

I walk some way down the street cluttered with cafes and bars and bric-a-brac shops until I find the small store opening. I'm holding a pair of black pumps with a heel missing and some sandals cracked down the spine.

Inside the store it is musty with the smell of leather and yeast and something darkly unexplained, like moss. On the counter is an old brass bell that I tap and it echoes through the shop.

Robert walks out, his glasses propped up on his head. Show me, he says, and I pass across my jumble of straps and leather and buckles, which he examines gently, like they are the shards of my glass slipper left behind at the ball. The tenderness makes me feel sad. He must have seen it because he looks at me and says, just to see you smile, I will knock off ten from the price.

How long have you been here? I ask, arranging my mouth into a smile.

Oh, for a long, long time. Before the place was like this and they got the poor people to move away so the big money could move in, he says, gesturing to the streets outside.

You still get good business even with all these new shops around?

Oh, sure. The area used to be very busy—it was filled with industry, breweries, glass works, and the police academy. There was a stage when the industry closed down in Redfern in the eighties through to the nineties where I was on the edge of going broke. But now again everyone comes here for their shoes because of the prices I charge. The Rabbitohs come, the women from those fancy beaches in the east, even James Packer once came here.

When was that? I ask.

He stops and looks at me over his glasses. You like asking questions, girl. You come back here on a Sunday when I have coffee and more time and I will answer your curiosity.

Lately, I have been asking strangers about their neighbourhoods. I am not sure if it is for work anymore, or if it just gives me reason to talk to strangers, even when I know nothing will come of my questions.

On the Sunday, I find myself with nothing to do, so I return to his shop. This time it's closed and I squeeze my hand through the metal grille on the door to rap against the glass. I hear music coming from inside and worry he can't hear me, and I try again, my knuckles grazing against the bars. Robert comes to the door, a cigarette in his mouth, and his beard has grown thicker since the beginning of the week.

Come in, come in, he says, ushering me into the back room.

Inside is a minimalist's nightmare. A wide wooden workbench is filled with hammers and vices and piles of cigarette smoke. A transistor radio is playing old Lebanese pop music. You heard this? he says, and turns it up louder. A bag of heel ends has been tipped onto the table.

This is George, he says, pointing to an old man who is sitting on the bench hammering at a piece of leather. The man looks up and nods and continues his hammering.

Here, here, Robert says, offering me a stool and dusting off the top. I perch on it as Robert and George smoke and examine the shoes strewn before them. Red leather boots, Converse sneakers, tan wedges, lace-ups, lilac mules.

Most of these are the simple jobs, he says, a loose heel or strap.

On the table are old tin vats of thick syrupy glue. From the horses, he says, nodding at it, and I recoil in horror, making him and George laugh.

Coffee? he asks and I nod before I see it is the powdered stuff. With all the cafes and artisanal coffee shops around them they still stick with this old paste. He dumps three sugars in without asking, pours in the boiling water from a kettle perched above wall hooks, along with a slug of long-life milk, and hands it to me.

I blow across the top to cool it down and ask when they came to Australia, trying to include George in the grand sweep of the question, but Robert appears to be the voice for the two of them.

We moved to Coogee from Lebanon in the forties during the war and then my father set up this shoe-repairs business. In sixty-four I took over the business and now I'm training up my twenty-year-old son to take over. You single? he asks. Shoe repairs can pay well on good days, he says with a wink.

Has the area changed much?

He and George look at each other and chuckle.

Everywhere has changed, sweetheart.

I remember when I was fifteen and I wanted to take a girl out from Paddington, says Robert, and a couple of people started laughing at me. They said 'Paddo'—it's a rubbish place. Her mother was a tram conductor and it was considered low level—now look at it.

All the white people moved out of here in the sixties, they wanted to go live the suburban dream. So, in came the Greeks, the Lebanese, the Yugoslavs, all of them, and they bought their houses in Redfern and painted everything mission brown, when it was cedar. All along Cleveland Street you can see the culture they brought with them, the restaurants like Fatima's and Abdul's. The place gets good again, so now back come the whites, and new people, and the doctors, and they strip away the brown, polish up the cedar, and now it's priceless. But that's good for my business and me, so we don't complain, eh George?

George grunts.

We try to stay out of the politics of these parts. We haven't had trouble from the Aboriginal people. But it's pretty clear what's going on. It's politics. They want the poor people to move away so the big money can move in. There's the new generation, these new people, and they don't want to live on the other side of the city. The government tried to build up Parramatta and make it like a city to convince people to move there instead. But every person I know, even policemen, they will come all the way from there because of the prices I charge, and they all say Parramatta is still Parramatta. You can get a donkey and dye his hair, cut his hair, thicken his mane, and put a saddle on him and he'll look like a horse—but he's still a donkey.

But we've seen things here over the years. Remember the fires, George? There were some buildings set alight but we know it was to get the money for insurance, cos we were here working late and saw the man come and pour the drums of petrol along the wooden beams. But we never said anything. Sometimes if you want to stay in a neighbourhood for a long time you have to learn to be quiet.

Now, the real question, he says, not looking up from the suede boot, is why are you spending your Sunday with two old men like us? What's wrong with you? You should be out with young men who are trying to buy you things and make you laugh, instead of sitting here with George and me and the horse glue. We're not complaining. And I think George likes your legs, eh George, but go on, get out of here, unless you came here to marry my son.

I have nowhere else to be and I can pretend to be someone else with strangers. But I don't say this, and instead roll my eyes playfully.

I drink my coffee as Robert and George smoke and cut and stitch and joke the whole time. I watch George strip the leather of the shoe back to the skeleton, so bare and exposed.

How do you keep your heart from breaking when you stand in the streets and know they will never go back to the way they were, is what I really want to ask him. How can you keep singing along to this old Lebanese pop music when everything around you is changing?

I watch Robert line up the finished pair of boots, tie a green price tag on them, and prop them up alongside the others, his work almost finished for the day.

I suddenly want him to rip out my insides and pour that thick smelly glue down my throat. I want to be cobbled and buttoned and stretched and magically put back together like these broken shoes.

I pick up my bag, shake their hands, and pretend to giggle when Robert jokingly goes in for a kiss while walking me towards the door.

Robert says, wait, and reaches up to one of the shelves, pulling down a plastic bag. Inside are my shoes. And he rips off the green price tag and says, this one is on us but next time you pay, and ushers me out the door.

12

Aleks and I sit in the car at Botany Bay. The airport lies across the stretch of water in front of us. We don't speak. Instead, we watch as the planes fly at low range over our heads, these giant and monstrous winged creatures showing off. Their turbo jets gently rattle the car windows.

Your grief, he says. It is too much for me. I need some time to think.

I remember New Year's Eve three years ago. We danced and skipped across Pyrmont Bridge. We ran into the folds of people at Darling Harbour, all eager to watch their year disappear with million-dollar lights exploding in the sky. Tummy-churning bass echoed off the party boats in the water. Girls in heels stumbled. Men in tight T-shirts pumped their fists.

I want to lick the salt off your eyebrows, I said, and leaned across with my tongue out, but he pushed me back, laughing, so my mouth just grazed his cheek.

Settle down, he said, and he winked. I looked at the sinews in his arms and the way his grey T-shirt rested softly on his collarbones.

We sat on his narrow balcony and listened, from a distance, with my head on his shoulder, as our island counted down the new year a day earlier than the rest of the world. And he held me close and told me to always keep a map of where I would go in this world, so he would know how and where to find me in the future. I hugged myself and thought of all the places we would go together.

*

We get up and walk along the pier in the light drizzle. The lights from the airport look murky and smudged; all the warning signs are drowned out by the rain. At the edge of the pier is a tumble of rocks with a plaque attached. It was here, at Kurnell Peninsula in 1770, that Captain Cook left the HMS *Endeavour* in a longboat and first set foot on Australian soil.

I read now silently from one of the plaques with a quote from Cook's journal about seeing Aboriginal people on the land.

> I thought that they beckoned us to come ashore, but in this we were mistaken, for as soon as we put the boat in they again came to oppose us. I fired a musket between the two which had no effect one of them took up a stone and threw at us

How can there be so much misunderstanding, Aleks murmurs, looking out to the water.

Beneath our wet jackets, our bones haven't yet learned how to let go, and he reaches out instinctively for my hand. We keep walking along the foreshore hand-in-hand, looking for more evidence of that first historical discovery.

13.

Eleven o'clock in the morning is the witching hour on Sydney's public transport. Everyone who lives outside of the city's routine hours jumps aboard and we trundle and clang out west together.

Hallelujah and thank you Jesus. This is my original song. I love you Dear Lord. Copyright twenty-nineteen. The Jesus preacher sits in the middle section.

She talks funny, a little girl whispers to her mum.

Old Vietnamese ladies sit with their tartan shopping trolleys tucked by their knees and pick and peel at sticky rice balls. Recently arrived immigrants from India play Bollywood tracks on tinny speakers on their old Samsungs. Groups of guys with their hats pulled backwards jump the train. They roam up and down the aisles, up and down, with such bravado, until a train guard kicks them off and their cries of fuck youuuuuuuu are lost on the tracks. Two teenage Samoan boys grind against the poles as their friend beatboxes. An old man sits in the corner, thin with agitation, and mutters angrily about prostitutes and how dark the world is becoming.

In a year, the hospital therapist told me, when I asked her when I'd feel better. In a year or so, she said, it will feel different.

The truth is in some ways, a year later, this part is almost harder. People rarely ask about it anymore. But grief still sits there alive and heavy in the belly.

Grief oozes from the pores and radiates outwards, so people

catch the scent on you. People swerve to avoid you on the foot-paths; they look for escape routes at parties. Strangers' eyes dart nervously when you speak, unclear of exactly what it is, but scared it is contagious.

Grief is invisible. It is an ice-cold sliver of dread that wakes you up every morning, which no amount of clothes can warm up. It's like a kid's game of catch your shadow. A flicker of something, trying to capture it and pull it back into yourself, recognition: that is me! But the more you chase yourself the harder you can be to grasp.

Grief catches me at unsuspecting moments and times. On this street. In that shop. In a turn of phrase. In this memory. It seeps into the grooves and cracks of a place. It doesn't obey a linear arc: it ducks and weaves. It dwells in the past, and as time moves forward, I find myself seeking refuge and solace, escaping into memories of growing up when the city felt famil-iar, like a friend, instead of this changing landscape with its new demands.

Back and forth, to and from interviews in various pockets of this city, I've learned to sit with my headphones on, so peo-ple stop approaching me.

Sometimes I sit on the trains with nothing playing, just lis-tening to the static around me: the chug of the train, and the wails and the stories of the commuters.

14

Over a year ago, I moved back to my childhood home. I had been lying on the floor of my old room for some hours, while family friends talked with my mum and dad in the kitchen. We had just found out his cancer was terminal, caused by the rapid production of abnormal white blood cells. These cells were no longer in harmony with the rest of his body. They were waging a war, not listening to the body's signposts and commands. There was no stop to it. No intersection. No give way.

I was meant to come out and join them. But my limbs had taken root. I was metamorphosing into a plant, I decided.

My dad came and stood at the doorway. Get up. They've all left. Let's go for a walk.

No, I'm all right, I mumbled at the ceiling.

I used to lie like this in the same room when I was a teenager, staring at posters of Jeff Buckley and Daniel Johns on my wall, irritated when my parents would call me for dinner.

For the first time my dad and I didn't know what to say to each other. We still had months, so it was hardly like we could say goodbye. But acting 'normal' was also no longer an option.

I had been spending the past weeks watching hours of *Planet Earth* documentaries in my darkened room, shutters down. I took strange comfort in watching the cycle of life and death play out in front of me as time slipped away.

No one in my world seemed to be able to talk about death.

It was a secret that we held inside while it corroded our organs, twisted our muscles.

I watched the vicious swoop of an eagle as it spotted a morsel running along the Mongolian tundra. The ruthless tricks played by the cuckoo bird, too lazy to build its own home and instead laying eggs that perfectly mimicked those of other birds and taking over their nests. I watched as the cuckoo was born and when it kicked out the remaining eggs, claiming its throne, I laughed. I watched them hatching, surviving, and dying. Only the birds seem to understand that the real world goes like this.

Come on, my dad said again, let's go around the block a couple of times.

I sighed heavily and rolled my eyes, like I was in the middle of something very important and he'd just asked me to take the garbage out.

Fiiiiiiine, I said, and then made a big show of picking my limbs up off the floor and dragging my feet towards the front door. He watched me but didn't say anything, while I cringed at the thought of myself.

We walked down the road in silence. It wasn't a bad silence. We weren't searching for something to say.

We found the lone bench at a small rocky park set on a steep incline, which I had walked past many times but never actually stopped at. I tried to temper myself to its hard edges. The grass was growing in patchy clumps and parts of it had yellowed and then browned from the dew. The seat was cold.

This is an ugly park, I said, and he asked me, do you want to go the main park? It's a longer walk though.

I said no and slumped further into the bench, and we both stared out at the nearby church, where some kids were practising fencing. They were running around wearing white netted helmets that made them look like little aliens.

He reached across and picked up my hand. He didn't say

anything. It was clear he also didn't know how to act. We just sat there for a while in the rocky park, holding hands, in a shared silence.

After some time, after the little kid–aliens had been picked up by their parents, we stood and wandered arm in arm back to the house, knowing that each day was going to be different from here on.

SUMMER

15.

W hat's the point of investing in nice things when everywhere we live is temporary? Bowerbird asks.

Summer is here and it is a Saturday afternoon and we are all home at the same time. We are drinking beers on our outdoor step overlooking the astroturf, which has had a lot of tropical rain lately and is looking less than lush.

Our house is not filled with nice things.

My room is set up with a simple bed, a bedside table, the wardrobe Aleks brought, and an extra hanging rack for my winter jackets. As a teenager and throughout university, I would stick up pictures of friends and family and pretty designs that I liked, and my whole room would look like a collage. Here, I leave the walls bare.

The walls in this house are Egyptian red, the same as a colouring pencil I owned as a kid. They were painted by one of the previous occupants and the colour has a closing-in effect.

Spots of mould have begun appearing on the bedroom walls and in the bathroom, and there is often one of us in the kitchen soaking a tea towel in white vinegar to rub them down. Sometimes the house smells like vinegar mixed with the patchouli we use in an attempt to cover up the smell of vinegar, and it can feel claustrophobic.

I've lived in so many share houses now, Niki says, and it is the same conversation; we don't want to plant herbs in the garden bed, or buy a quality kitchen table, because who knows when we will have to move on. I lived with a guy who had a really nice set of carving knives. And he brought them to the share house, but, you know, they weren't treated with the respect they probably deserved. Day after day we used them to cut things they weren't made for and over time they became blunt. He would sharpen them. But the same thing kept happening until one day he got upset and hid them, and said he would never bring nice things to the share house ever again.

Bowerbird is idly tuning his guitar. He says he will buy nice furniture when he has his own house to put it in.

Sami raises an eyebrow, takes a sip of beer, and looks amused. You might be waiting a lifetime, he says.

Judging by the market projections, Sami doesn't see how he could afford to buy anything in the next ten years, even out in the suburbs near his parents.

Niki, Bowerbird, and I exchange looks. None of us really talk about how much money we earn, but we have a feeling Sami earns more than he lets on. So it is surprising, almost scary, to hear that even he doesn't feel confident he will be able to buy a home.

We only know what each other earns in the most abstract way. Sami, we assume, must earn decent money, because he is in corporate law and owns three designer suits and has the biggest room in the house, the upstairs one with the full balcony.

Niki and I suspect Bowerbird comes from wealth or has someone supporting his lifestyle as he buys all organic food and expensive cured meats and then leaves them to rot in the fridge. He never mentions money as a motivation behind any of his choices, which means he must have some.

Niki meanwhile is constantly stressed about money, and talks about it in an abstract way that revolves around lack. I don't know how much of it is that she needs money and how much is from the fear of not having money. This dictates her choices and she picks up more jobs than anyone I know. I don't know how she finds the hours or the energy or what any of them really entail, but she always has side hustles.

When the four of us get together, we all talk openly about our wants and even seem to have similar types of dreams. Travel, accumulating experiences, a home in a city with our friends and family, and how we want to chase the sun around this globe. But none of us ever talk directly about the means with which we can chase that sun.

There is a shame in not having enough, in being the one who doesn't pay their round at the pub, or who never hosts a dinner, or who hasn't travelled. But there is also something shameful about having money, a savings plan, shares, and those who have it rarely seem to let on.

I am getting by on my freelance work, but I know it is not a way of working that can last. I can afford my rent, groceries, coffee, and the occasional cheap dinner out. At the markets, I will let myself splurge on earrings, scented organic soaps, and bound leather notebooks. Some nights I wake up with a feeling of dread about the future and money. Then I try to make promises to myself that the next day I will push my life into some kind of shape, but when I wake up, I am exhausted.

Sami says the bubble has to burst soon. But even then, with a burst bubble, he is not sure how much it will change things for us.

The question, says Bowerbird, waving his hand mystically, is whether the bubble is even real, and he plucks a dramatic chord on his guitar.

Niki says it depresses her, all this talk of how to buy a house.

I hate being suckered in by the media's hysteria, she says, but it really does feel like none of us will ever be able to afford to live in the city we grew up in. Surely there should be special rates given to people who have experienced falling in love and heartbreak and birth and death in one place? Isn't that true ownership anyway?

Maybe what we need is to treat the temporary more like this is our real life. You know, start by investing in the here and now, says Sami.

Bowerbird nods and plucks a few more chords. That's a pretty damn nice statement, it's almost Buddhist of you, Sami.

But none of us actually have the money, or want to fork out the money, to buy furniture and end up like the guy with the carving knives.

We could paint the walls, Niki suggests after a while. I'm sure the landlord wouldn't mind and it could be just enough to make it feel like ours for a bit?

We all agree this is a brilliant idea. It fits our budget, and would disguise the mould and the doomsday Egyptian red.

Bowerbird plays the beginnings of a little Spanish melody while we decide it should be a pale yellow, like the sun.

And while we get excited about it and clink our beers on this summer afternoon, like most dreams, we put it off for another day.

16

I am on the train heading out to Homebush to do an interview. I remember being on the same train when I was eleven with my dad one hot, sticky afternoon. I was returning home in disgrace. I had been at the new home of my childhood friend Mariella, who had recently moved after her parents split up. She was the first one whose parents got a divorce, and we were all scared it would spread across the grade, like a domino effect, so we kept close track of our parents' movements.

Mariella had invited a few of us girls to her father's, which was far away. But there was a pool, so we said yes. They lived in a complex of houses, which all looked identical, so different from her artist mum's house with its wacky sculptures, hanging plants, and black-and-white photographs on the walls. The hedges were cut at an even height and everything was blindingly white.

When we arrived, I put my new pink sunglasses on and felt cool, while my dad shook his head and said, gated community. It made me think of a book I was reading about a girl who was locked in a commune and I felt sort of panicky, but I couldn't say anything, because I knew I wasn't allowed to read books like that. I had also read a book about a girl who wrote letters to her penpal, but halfway through realised the other girl was in a maximum-security prison and had a violent brother who smacked her on the tits. I was so scared that I told my dad, and he got mad and threw the book outside. It was raining, and in the morning the pages had stuck together. I never found out if the girl lived or died.

I didn't want to put my dad in a bad mood. It was one of those days he needed to just be on his own. We called them sea-creature days, he and I. It was the name we gave to those dark shapes that churned and threatened to close in.

Is it a sea-creature day? I would say to him. And he might smile, a small smile, and nod his head. Yes, he would say.

What kind?

A seal, he might say, and on those days, he would pinch my nose. We might go out for a walk, or to one of his favourite cafes, and I knew I could make him feel better.

A squid, he might say at other times, or an octopus, and on those days, I would disappear to my room and try to be quiet and small.

Those were the times he would sit at his desk, head buried, writing furiously, and I imagined the dark ink pouring out of his fountain pen and wrapping around his mind like tentacles. Those days were nothing to be feared, but I remember tiptoeing out of his study, knowing I no longer occupied a space in his thoughts, and I felt left behind as he went to the invisible places in his imagination. I knew it wasn't supposed to make me upset, but it did anyway. I would feel myself dissolving a little, unsure how to create sharp, real contours around my own day.

We rang the bell and Mariella opened the door, and I said goodbye to my dad, who kissed me, but I felt his mind swirl away as he turned.

Inside, the carpet was so thick I almost sank into an off-white sea. We went out to the pool. There were four other girls there and we began to play Surf Life Savers, where one of us would pretend to drown so we could practise swimming on our backs with their deadweight, and then pretend to give CPR. On other visits we'd played a game we called mermaids, where we swam around making weird ocean sounds and swallowed too much chlorine. And another game where we would push our vulvas against the jets in the pool and scream and laugh and ask each other if we felt anything.

But all our games, here and at school, were starting to be replaced by long talks about boys, and who would wear a pad or be brave enough to try a tampon. The girls had started buying crop tops, and comparing the make and model and the shades of cream, and beige, and lily whites. Only one girl, Carla Romanello, had bought a bra, and all I knew as I saw the greedy way the boys watched her and laughed as she jiggled past them, was that I never wanted them to look at me like that; I never wanted a bra. I just wanted to make underwater ocean sounds.

So, when the others sat by the side of the pool drinking cordial and signalling that game time was over and it was time to begin talking about Peter Reynolds in grade six, I decided to distract them by doing funny flips off the side of the pool. I tried somersaults. They kept talking. I tried bombing loudly so it would splash on them. But they kept talking. I called out to Mariella, who normally couldn't resist showing off what she learned at gymnastics class, and although she looked torn, she stayed sitting and I saw her whisper something while the others rolled their eyes.

I knew it was about me, but I pretended not to care. I got a bucket and filled it with water, and while they were busy talking about their crushes, I dumped it over Mariella's head and she screamed. She stood up and glared at me. Grow up, she said with something close to disgust.

I tried to pinpoint the moment everything turned into upside-down-land and thought maybe I could reverse it by doing a backflip, so I took a running leap towards the pool, but my foot slipped, and I landed with a dull thud on the ground instead of in the water.

They stopped talking.

Mariella got her dad, who was a chiropractor and made me lie still on the cold orange bricks. He asked me if I could raise different parts of my body, then turned me slowly onto my stomach and sat on me to crack my back, while my whole body buckled under his weight and made a crunching sound. Although I felt fine, he said he would call my dad to come and get me. I told him not to, as I knew the girls would tease me later, but her dad shook his head. I was told to sit inside and wait with cordial while the girls went back into the pool to talk.

When my dad arrived, his feet also sank into the carpet, and his face was rumpled as he asked me in front of everyone why I had done something so stupid. We walked to the train station in silence. It was only on the train that he grudgingly spoke to me to ask if I wanted to play the spelling game.

We were in the middle of 'discombobulated' when a woman walked up the steps, shouting. She was all tight and sinewy. She kept swearing and I was embarrassed because I knew I wasn't supposed to know the words that were giving me a thrill.

You dirty fucking cocksucker you fucking rag-munching piece of scum.

She was yelling this disjointedly to no one in particular.

But then she started lurching along the carriage towards us. I was sitting by the window and my dad was the closest to her on the aisle. Suddenly she was standing over him and screaming at him.

You fucking piece of filth how could you do this to me you fucking fucker?

He kept staring straight ahead like he hadn't heard her. This made her angrier, and made me nervous, and now her whole body was convulsing in accusation. Down her arm were thick scars like rope.

I'll kill you motherfucker.

You, she said, leaning in close to us with her sour breath. In the crook of her fingers she was holding a bottle of wine.

She lifted her arm and the bottle with it. I watched, horrified. No one in the train carriage moved and I wondered if they, too, were thinking about what my dad had done to this woman. My fingers dug into my thighs. The bottle started to come down towards his head and her face was so small and so screamy and so knotted, and he was just sitting there not moving. I'm not sure if I shouted. But I saw the bottle was about to smash onto his head when he suddenly, at the last minute, held his arms out and gently gripped her wrists.

She screamed, I'm going to find where you live you fucker and cut up your daughter's face, while my dad sat there and spit was bouncing out of her mouth.

Please leave us alone, he said quietly.

That seemed to mobilise everyone on the train, and they got up to help my dad escort the woman, thrashing, down the train stairs. The doors of the train opened at a station, and she got out, still screaming into the chamber of the train until the door closed.

How do you know her? I whispered when he got back and sat down next to me. He just shook his head.

Then why did she say those things to you, and why did she want to hit you, and why weren't you scared, and why did you just sit there, I wanted to ask. Suddenly, every interaction between every single person in the world felt so heavy. Everyone had these needs and thoughts churning, every single day, and I didn't understand how you were supposed to keep up with all of it.

I burst into tears, scared that this woman would find him and hurt us like she'd been hurt, those thick, hot lines crisscrossing down her arms.

He brushed my forehead, and said that sometimes people want to find someone to blame because the insides of their bodies feel like prisons.

Is that why you go away and write to catch your thoughts, I asked, so they don't drag you away?

Yes, sort of, he said. You know how sometimes you get so many worries about things changing, or you have thoughts that feel a bit crazy that no one will understand? I nodded. It's important to find somewhere to put all of the upset, he said, so you don't become like that poor woman and take it out on the wrong people.

It was strange to realise sometimes things got too much for him too.

It will be okay, he said, ruffling my hair and pretending to pinch off my nose.

I look out of the window now, at all the Asian stores flashing past, and I think about the jerking woman with all her stretchy cuts, and her glass stare, and how all of us have sea creatures swimming in our heads, and I feel sad that she had no one to talk with, like I did, to make her pain fall away.

17.

B owerbird is trying to find a candle that smells like the ocean and I am coming along for the ride. He tells me he has already tried three different batches and they all ended up smelling like soap, so we are on our way to a warehouse to collect batch number four.

The warehouse is out at Tempe, and we drive past IKEA and the giant tip, and flinch as trucks hurtle and honk alongside us.

All the candle shops go too heavy on the base smell and patchouli, he tells me. The floral overtones can really kill it.

He is planning the launch party for his new EP and already our house has become a dumping site for his ideas: posters, guitar leads, bed frames, wicker chairs, and the discarded blue, soapy candles that I keep finding tucked behind the toilet or in between sofa seats.

You should get insurance on that nose of yours, I tell him. People do that, you know, like in perfumeries.

His sister has just been told she is ill, with cancer like my father had, but they found it earlier and it is in a different part of her body, so there is hope. In the car we talk about episodes of *Louie*, the morality of consuming art by misogynists, how fucked up CrossFit people are, the candles: everything except what is happening to his sister.

When I ask him why he wants the smell of the ocean, he says everyone loves the ocean, and he wants people to walk into his launch and think of their childhood, and summer, and feel okay again.

Every day I listen as Bowerbird practises chords on his guitar in the badly soundproofed room below mine, until the sound rings in my ears. A hologram shimmer settles around both of our bodies, which sometimes makes others feel uneasy in our company.

Sometimes, like today, Bowerbird is the only person I want to be around. Not because we talk about it, but because I recognise the same traces of gunmetal blue bruising up underneath his eyes with the relentless silent question: how can you lose so much?

He misses the turn-off and we spend the next fifteen minutes negotiating our way across intersections dense with traffic. We circle back and find the driveway to the warehouse.

There is a tiny makeshift counter at the front and an elderly man with a stern look, aggressive eyebrows, and a nametag, 'Massimo', who asks Bowerbird brusquely what he ordered. Bowerbird gives the docket to Massimo, who sighs and walks to the back, and we look through the front window as a truck tries to reverse into a narrow space and almost squashes a car.

Massimo comes back carrying a cardboard box.

Ah, he says, the ocean one, thumping it onto the counter. This one was a bit tricky. And suddenly his scowl clears and he says, it's hard to get something so light and salty, that's more like a feeling, and put it into a scent.

We look at each other, surprised, and I giggle at this man's sudden poetry. Massimo's face shuts down again.

The box is packed with bubble wrap. We pull out the stuffing in the car park, bursting the air pockets in loud gleeful bangs. Bowerbird picks up one of the candles, which is short and fat in its glass dish, and a vivid, unnatural blue.

This doesn't bode well, he says as he leans down to smell. It smells like soap.

Maybe Massimo is right after all, it's too hard to capture a feeling, he says, as he throws the candle back into the bubble wrap in disgust, where it will go on to join the other discarded candles scattered around our house.

18

My father was not actually of the ocean. His elemental quality was more earth, rock, and soil, and the steady metronome of walking footsteps.

I think he was embarrassed by some of the fathers who flashed their bodies around at the surf. But one time, when I was thirteen and just in high school, we went on a trip together, just the two of us, to the south coast.

The south coast of New South Wales has a wilderness; it's like the tearaway cousin that reminds the manicured Sydney city beaches of their true rough potential.

We caught the train and it wound around past Scarborough, and Coledale, and all the towns nestled on the cliffs along the coal coast towards Wollongong. Wollongong was named by the Dharawal and one translation is 'song of the sea.' The region had once enjoyed Australia's coal boom, with Wollongong as the district's thriving port town and industrial centre. But when the economy went into recession in the eighties, the town was gutted and the streets smelled of boredom, while the chimneys coughed up dark, useless smoke, until, decades later, the town spluttered to life again.

We stayed in a room above an old pub. When we walked in the smell of stale beer hit us, old men holding schooners and braless women looked up and stared, and I tensed. But my father was at ease—this was his scene growing up—and his comfort made me relax my shoulders.

That evening we walked across the sand to the one restaurant in town, an Italian joint with chequered plastic tablecloths that flapped in the sea breeze, and gulls crowded around our feet.

It was at the dinner, while we were twirling pasta and talking about the ocean, that he told me about a different kind of sea creature.

These creatures were part-woman, part-seal, and they lured sailors to the rocks.

How did they become like that? I asked, looking out to the sea.

They were seals during the day when they would play and jump in the waves, like you were doing today, he said. But at night, they would pull themselves onto the rocks and shed their seal skins and take their human form.

They could be two things at once, I said, mesmerised by the idea that something could exist between two worlds.

Except, when men found out about their secret, he said, they would steal their skins and hide them, so they had to remain on land as women forever. They would marry and have children with the men. But they would always listen to the ocean. It would call them. Even while they nursed their infants, they could hear the song. In some stories, they would discover where their skins were hidden, and they would slip their pelts back on and disappear into the waves, and their husbands and children could never find them again.

This was around the time I noticed my own body start to change. The changes sometimes felt like thick, unwanted new skin. I felt a tearing. My body ached. I tried desperately to keep these changes a secret. I didn't want anything to change between my father and me.

19

We have decided to put up a Christmas tree in the house, but a fake one, as Niki says it's bad for the environment otherwise.

Well, so is this plastic thing from the two-dollar shop, Bowerbird points out.

I am surprised it is Christmas. Christmas has always been salty hair and swimming costumes, hot chips and Golden Gaytime ice creams against the backdrop of the ocean and the cricket on the radio, as the days stretched out longer and hotter. Even though the shop windows have rolled out their displays and people are talking about their holidays, nothing feels familiar.

None of us are doing much for Christmas this year. My mum is still away and hasn't said anything to me about when, or if, she will be returning. She just says she needs to be away from this city and the memories, and to feel closer to her home.

But this is your home, I want to say, and I am here. I wonder if she's also forgotten it's Christmas.

Niki doesn't have the money to travel back to see her family this year, Sami's family doesn't celebrate it, and Bowerbird shrugs his shoulders and says he can't be bothered.

Bowerbird says we can have an Orphan's Christmas instead, and I see Niki look towards me and pinch him, and he says, ow, what was that for?

Shall we do a Kris Kringle, Niki suggests.

What is that, asks Sami, and Bowerbird almost explodes.

How could you not know?

Sami shrugs his shoulders and says he usually lays low around Christmas time. He says he wasn't a part of some of these things as a child, and so the habit of not asking grew, until he either became disinterested or it was too late to ask.

Christmas was kind of a lonely time for me, he says. My parents didn't get it, my sisters were too young, and so I just avoided those conversations at school. You just learn to fit in, you know, and you don't think beyond that goal. So, I get the term, but yeah, like, what the fuck actually is a Kris Kringle?

Bowerbird starts explaining it to him: we all put our names into a bowl, and then we draw a name out and you don't tell anyone but that is who you buy a present for. He taps the table in a little beat to end on a flourish while Sami looks expectantly for him to continue.

Oh, that's it? My childhood trauma at being left out was over that?

Bowerbird pauses and says, yeah, it's actually pretty anticlimactic after all.

We add a couple more people who will also be around to the list, like Bowerbird's cafe girlfriend and Andy, and decide to cap the cost of the present at twenty-five dollars.

I pull out Sami's name. It makes me a little nervous as I know he likes nicer things and I am not sure what to buy for a guy who has style.

The next day, I wander into a department store to look for his gift. Carols play on a loop, the store is ablaze with artificial lights, and in the windows robotic elves and magical creatures shriek with laughter.

Loneliness is not something we should feel any longer in this age of constant connection, and we feel cheated when the signs reveal themselves. We crush its existence, trample its edges. No dwelling. We maniacally search for the next work opportunity. We swipe right and drink and push up against someone to fill that gap. We try to move quickly past death and loss. Each time something ends, we fill the space with distractions before we have a moment to pause.

But what does that do to us, when we are never allowed to exhale? How do we keep breathing?

I see a pair of dice cufflinks on a stand in the men's accessories section. They are a fancier version of the ones I bought at the garage sale when I first met Sami, and I decide this will do, there is a joke in there somewhere, and I buy them for his Kris Kringle.

20

W e were always late to Christmas events. The late family.

My parents would get caught up and distracted by whatever was happening in the moment. A phone call, a disagreement, reading the newspaper, listening to music; time did not seem like a factor in my parents' preparations.

It drove me crazy.

Every second year, we celebrated with my father's side of the family and it was essential for me to be there on time so I could carve out my place among my cousins.

They would already be at my grandmother's, picking up their presents from under the tree and shaking them, and planning the rules for games of backyard cricket and chasings to follow. I wanted to be among it. But neither of my parents bought into the fuss of Christmas, my mother because her family was Hindu, and my father because it was, he said, capitalist nonsense.

I was often in awe of friends' families, with their houses almost choked by Christmas trees and tinsel, and I craved the frantic, energetic force of celebration and getting things done.

In the alternate years, we would visit my Indian side in Sydney, and sit indoors in the cool air conditioning, the cricket on in the background, while the adults talked about how what was happening in India was no good. They used words like nationalism and separatists, shaking their heads, and ate dosas and drank mugs of thick black coffee, while my other cousins and I jumped around, impatient to play outside among the eucalyptus trees in the sun.

My parents' love, I knew, had something to do with those words too, as they were often spoken in our family home while I was growing up. My mother and father had first met at a political rally, at a time when war was raging over Kashmir in the north and Marxism was flourishing in the south. My father had lived in India for a long period in his twenties and felt strongly about both issues, and my mother was searching for a way to reconnect with something vital in her homeland, here, in this other country.

One Christmas morning, we were heading to my father's side of the family and things were taking even longer than usual. I was beside myself and I peeked into their bedroom, desperate to know what was holding them up this time.

I saw them in bed, coiled together, my father with one arm wrapped underneath my mother's head, propping it up like a pillow, and the other hand holding a book of verse.

He was reading poetry aloud as her hands traced the outlines of his words in the air and her eyelids fluttered closed. It felt so intimate that I pulled back sharply and sat on the floor of the corridor, listening to these words coming from their room.

Years later, I looked up this poet and the words my father was speaking to my mother.

They belonged to a Kashmiri-American poet, Agha Shahid Ali, who could never return to his own homeland and wrote year after year of that longing.

That Christmas, I crept slowly back to my room, understanding that my parents had their own secret world. Their lives didn't go on pause when I wasn't there. I felt both betrayed by this knowledge and a thrill at the thought of this vast land that existed beyond myself. They had some language that I didn't understand, and perhaps never would.

As I sat on my bed and dangled my legs, I knew all I could do, for now, was wait.

21

On a Saturday evening, I am on the train to a friend's place and an old man with a long beard and a six-pack of beer sits alone in the middle landing, drinking. He has a big garbage bag at his feet, which seems to contain his belongings.

At Central Station, a group of three young men get on, all backward-capped and restless and jangly with bravado, scoping out the train, and their eyes land on the old man.

Hey, Father Christmas, they say playfully, what are you doing out at this time?

The old man wheezes and laughs and raises his beer in a sign of cheers.

What are you drinking for, old man?

The boys move in, towering over him, holding on to the poles while he sits. It seems a little too close.

Yeah, why you drinking on a train alone on a Sunday night, Father Christmas?

Father Christmas looks a little confused. He laughs again and holds up the pack and asks if they want a beer.

We don't want your fucking beer, man, one of them says. He hits the can out of Father Christmas's hand, and it rolls across the floor of the train.

Okay settle boys, the man says, but it's slurred, because he is drunk and can't get the shape of the words right. The air in the carriage tightens.

You're stinking up this carriage, old man, says a different boy. Haven't you got anywhere else to go?

A woman looks around and opens her mouth to say something, but she shuts it again quickly when one of the boys says, cunt, and shoves his fingers up in a violent V shape, sticking his tongue through it at her. No one else moves.

Where the fuck is your family, or did you piss everything away, eh?

One of them grabs the garbage bag out of his hand, and when the man protests feebly, pushes him roughly back into the seat. The old man is too drunk and so he slips and bangs his head awkwardly against the pole, slumping back onto the seat.

You're fucking pathetic, says one boy, kicking the can that is rolling back and forth along the carriage floor.

And then the train stops and they jump off, charged up, laughing and hollering Merry Christmas, and disappear into the black evening.

22

I always feel like I'm about to take flight when I walk across the Anzac Bridge. Its cables stretch over the water like wings and it hangs suspended, its peaks swallowed up by the sky on cloudy days. People walk their dogs off leash along the bay, rowers shout out and do sprints back and forth, and girls in capris and floaty white shirts slide back into their glass-facade apartments.

In high school we used to come down to Blackwattle Bay to smoke bongs. The bay wasn't so pretty back then. It was all dug up and giant quarries of sand potholed the landscape. When we arrived, the boys from the local schools would set down their Nautica backpacks with great importance. They would pull out lighters and pop-top juice bottles, burn a hole into the side to melt the plastic, wedge the pipe piece into the hole and begin packing the cone.

I wasn't really in with any of these guys. I would sometimes tag along if one of the girls from school said she was going. I was intimidated by all the fussing and didn't know how to punch a bong properly.

But one time I got a special invite.

I think it was meant to be a date. It was the first time I had been asked anywhere by a guy, and he had found my number, and rung me, and I was nervous. I brought along my best friend, Tessa, who went to one of the Catholic all-girls schools and knew all about dating, and who had already been fingered by three guys. We got ready at her house and she tried to put her make-up on me, but nothing looked right, and she laughed, saying how come there was no foundation in my colour anyway.

The boy knew a special place to smoke. We skidded down to the other side of a quarry, climbed up an overhanging tree to another escarpment, and crawled to a small cave near the lapping waters. We didn't speak much as he packed the cone. Then he put his arm around me and showed me how to inhale the musty smoke. We lay back as our heads filled up. I don't know how much time passed, but when I looked over he was stroking the blonde strands of Tessa's hair and she was giggling into his shoulder. The cave suddenly felt very small. The water sounded like it was coming inside. My mouth was pasty and I had no idea where we were. I stumbled to my feet and said I needed water. They both giggled like they shared a secret, like they knew something I didn't. I tried to walk out of the cave but the water was so close. I started to slip down the tree. I landed with a thud into the quarry. Behind me I heard their shouts. Fuck her, I thought, with her blonde hair and her secrets and her matching make-up.

I stood up. For a moment I was alone in a crater, in the middle of the earth. Layers of sand and sediment had built up over the years, wet with colour. I could die here, I thought, and the grainy sand would fill my nostrils, my earholes, fill my mouth so I could no longer speak, and eventually my eye sockets would be replaced by earth and I would be part of this quarry forever. I stared up at the bridge floating high above me, offering possibilities and ways to get out that I didn't yet know how to reach.

I needed water. I started crawling up the other side of the quarry. I heard Tessa and the boy yelling behind me and tried to move quicker. I came to a little house at the top of the hill. They were getting closer, running up the slope.

I knocked on the door. An elderly lady opened it.

I need some water, please. I wasn't sure if my mouth was saying this but my head was screaming it at her and I hoped she understood. She looked around outside and then took me into her house. She asked me what I had taken. Even though I hated the others at that moment, I didn't want to get anyone in trouble and become an outcast at school so I told her I'd bought weed from some local boys on the street. She started telling me something about her daughter who got addicted to something bad after she started dating some boy from the Glebe housing flats, but I wasn't really following, and it didn't have anything to do with me. Finally, she gave me some water and a brown paper bag to breathe into. She called the ambulance and told me I had to ring my parents. The others hid outside. Behind them the bridge quivered. I sat on her couch, breathing in and out of the paper bag, waiting for everyone to arrive. I watched it expand and crush inwards, trying hard not to think about the trouble I would be in, or if I would ever be kissed, or how some girls knew how to have secrets with boys, or about the sand filling my earholes.

The construction ended some years later. Bulldozers moved the giant slabs of quarry, and filled up the earth, and the seeping water, with cement. Since that day I have come down to the bay many times. I have jogged here in the early morning, eaten plates of oysters at The Boathouse restaurant with Aleks, and listened as a man who walks along the foreshore, muttering numbers to himself, quietly tells me he counts the buses that trundle across the bridge, afraid he will one day miss a beat.

23.

I am meant to meet my housemates at a friend's apartment to drink and watch the floats, but it is on the other side of Anzac Parade, and even though it is still light, the floats have begun, and now it is impossible to cross the road. All I can see are feathers, skin and glitter. Summer is in full swing and the crowds push and pull and men adjust their wigs slipping in the growing humidity. I ask the policeman at the barricades where we can cross. A few other people come over to ask the same question. There is a couple dressed in polyvinyl bondage clothes—the woman is holding a whip. And there is a lively, handsome man wearing a small backpack. The policeman shakes his head and points down the street and tells us we'll have to keep walking.

I skip along with the handsome man, who is Italian and fun and funny, and everyone is in a flirty mood and we laugh weaving through the crowd to find the crossover point. The couple teases us and asks us if we want to be whipped.

I remember coming to Mardi Gras once in my twenties, late at night when the crowd was thinning and everyone was so drunk they were beginning to sober up again. Tessa kept walking up to strangers, begging to be spanked, leaning over in the middle of the road and pulling up her dress, giggling. We sat in the gutter to wait for her, among empty bottles and ribbons. Finally, a giant man in a leather mask with chains hit her with a paddle over and over, and as we all laughed and whooped I saw a strange look come over her face; she was quietly crying.

The woman cracks the whip hard against the bitumen and the Italian man swears in surprise, and then laughs and grabs my hand to run away.

We don't tell each other our names or why we're here or what we do. Instead we talk about the best ways to wash off glitter and who is more gay, Putin or Berlusconi.

A group comes towards us dressed in bright wigs and holding a flag that says Bi-Party. We ask them who they have come as and they tell us they have come as famous bisexuals: David Bowie, says one man, pointing to each member of the group, Marilyn Monroe, Julius Caesar.

Julius! I exclaim, and he says, oh, honey, all those Roman guys were, because in those days they didn't have any of that shit. What shit, I ask, and he says, you know, labels.

And who are you supposed to be, asks the Italian, and the man flashes a smile and says, you clearly don't know your *Star Wars*. I'm the ultimate queer hero, Obi-Wan Kenobi.

The Italian and I dance off, and try to remember if it's weed then beer that makes you freak out, or the other way around.

Beer and grass you're on your ass, grass and beer . . . I sing, but I can't remember the rest. We pass the Captain Cook Hotel on the corner, packed with people cheering and dancing. We still have a long way to go until we are able to cross the road, so we look at each other and squeeze into the bar to buy a bottle of vodka and some tonic. I swipe a couple of plastic cups lying on the counter and we squeeze back out, mixing our concoction and toasting our cups to the sky, which is darkening.

We're surrounded by muscles, all oiled-up and rippling. I tell the Italian he is wearing too many clothes and he should take his T-shirt off. He tells me my shoes don't suit my personality.

They are too clunky, he says. You're lighter and strappier than you believe. You need to get rid of these shoes.

I look down at my feet and I'm not sure whether to be offended or flattered. I fill our cups with more vodka and we keep walking, moving further and further away from the parade.

We pass a huge Moreton Bay fig tree leaning out from Centennial Park.

Let's go climbing, I shout. We run over the grass towards the tree. He helps push me up to the lower branches and then neatly pulls himself up with just one athletic arm. I clap for him. We sit with our feet hanging down, sipping our drinks. The parkland stretches out in front of us, and we hear a bird cry somewhere in the distance.

In the growing silence, he tells me his name, why he moved to Australia and how his father doesn't approve, and how he is saving to start his own business here if his visa comes through, and how, sometimes, he finds it so unbearably lonely to be here, on the other side of the world, away from everything.

I think about the Gay Pride banners nearby, and the dykes on bikes, and the silver spandex hot pants, and I want to be back in that bubble. I don't want to talk to this boy about his fears. This is the night where we all dress up and use hair spray and wear glittered masks and pretend to be the best versions of ourselves, without troubles or concerns. Where we don't talk about interior worlds, or how we have been hurt.

Or how when my mum calls now, there are long silences on either side of the phone. Neither of us seems to know what to say, and I put the phone on speaker as I wander around the house, aimlessly picking up objects, and let time drag between us and across oceans.

This is the night the city pretends to be someone else. And I think about why Tessa cried that night years ago in the middle of the road when her own mask slipped off and how a truth was revealed to everyone.

We leave the tree and start walking back to the parade where we are now allowed to cross. Confetti pumps out of powered guns from the floats and pieces of gold fall into our hair. The Italian lingers for a moment. And then he turns, and I watch him disappear, with his small backpack and his worries, into the sparkly crowd.

24

The sky is screaming. My house is screaming. The house across the road is screaming. Wait. It is a man screaming. I blink, disoriented and foggy, and look at my clock. It is 7 A.M. The shouting normally starts at night. But this is different, it is morning and it is screaming, and so I crawl out of bed.

My window is wide open behind the white cotton curtain. The air is thick and sticky at night. I still haven't set up a fly-screen to keep out the night-time mosquitoes and I have welts on my arm. From my vantage point behind the curtain I can see the whole street stretched out before me.

The man is screaming and squirming on the ground. Another man is standing over him, holding him down. And another man is swinging his arm. I watch, or I hear, a hollow crack. The man kicks him in the stomach. Again, and again, and again.

Some people are dogs, the police tell me later at the station, when I am asked to give a statement. We are always having problems with that house, the policeman says, at least some good things will come from this lot getting moved.

He wants to know how many punches before the man was knocked out. They want to know details because of the 'one-punch' laws. They tell me it is eight years in jail if the victim is killed by one punch. These laws, they say, are going to stop the growing problem of male violence in this city. They ask about our screaming neighbours, and they ask again how many punches.

The week before, a television crew came to our street to film a drama series. They want to show modern stories of Indigenous families who live in the area. Nikki, Sami, Bowerbird, and I hung off Sami's balcony, smoking roll-up cigarettes. We watched the actors and the crew as they floodlit the road, and we laughed with excitement. It was our little Hollywood moment, and as we caught the eye of our neighbours we waved, emboldened by the cameras.

This is a street, like so many others, that has an infamous House Across the Road. The house that is discussed with a sigh. This is a house about which we have conversations at our Sunday dinners, saying we care, because there are kids, and what about them, as we count the 'cunts' and the 'fucks' and the crashes coming from across the road, but really, deep down, all we want is some quiet sleep that isn't troubled by their pain.

25.

When I was in high school and best friends with Tessa, the world existed without fathers, or mothers, or family, as we wrapped each other up in our teenage myths. Where every curve of the street held a potential excitement, and it felt like no one but us could possibly understand what we felt, and so we used to hold on firmly to each other and navigate the city like it was our own secret world and only we had the code. That world later became populated with men, and relationships, and careers. It can be hard to imagine we existed in a world so tight and immediate.

We snuck out of Tessa's window in St. Peters one night to reach the party held by the older boys at the park with the abandoned chimney stacks. I drank vodka straight from the bottle, choking, my nostrils flaring.

We made up our own language and spoke in tongues through the night, never missing a beat. We held our half-moon friendship necklaces close to our chests.

She asked me what would make her more kissable. I told her to wear her hair down more often.

I asked her what razor she used, because her legs were always so silky. Venus, she said, and I made a mental note to stop stealing my dad's disposables that nicked me deep and bloody on the shin and to buy one of those instead.

She asked how far I'd gone. I was embarrassed and said I hadn't gone all the way but that I liked this guy who caught the 3.15 train and I'd totally do it with him, but I was scared. I asked her, and even though she was more experienced, she laughed and shrieked, same, she was scared, scared, scared.

We both hugged each other because we knew what it felt like to hide parts of ourselves.

I told her I was jealous of how confident and at ease she always seemed with people and how she knew what to say. Some time passed and she told me that her mum loved her sister more than her.

After another slug of the bottle, she told me sometimes she disliked me. She said that I reminded her of her sister, especially the way I laughed when I was with boys, and it made her want to scratch me on the face. I felt shaky and said nothing.

We stood up and walked towards the thick band of people moving heavily to bush doof music in the distance, the firefly glow of cigarette ends guiding us.

There were some older boys there, ones we'd never seen before. Two guys had spiky dark hair, and one had an eyebrow ring, and she whispered to me she thought he was cute, and that he looked like that guy from the TV show we watched about skater boys in high school, and she said she would totally do it with him.

They offered us their vodka, scrunched up in brown paper bags. They told us they felt old, like toolies. I laughed loudly, and she glared at me.

We took long sips. Tessa turned to say something to me, but suddenly my head was swimming with the noise, and I couldn't remember how to speak our language anymore.

The eyebrow-ring guy leaned in towards me and started to whisper in my ear all the things he liked about my hair, and my skin, and my top, and I saw her face flash before me, angry and confused. I went to say something to her but then his tongue was down my throat, and it was thick and pasty and took up all the space. When I looked up she was gone. I was alone with him.

I chattered nonsense to keep the fear at bay and told him about how one day I wanted to move to New York, and that I wanted to be an actress, and that I understood it was a difficult path, but I had never felt so alive as when I was on a stage. He murmured and said he could see it. And that he would come and visit. He said this as his hands moved firmly across my body.

I could still hear the thud of music in the distance, and I knew this was what people did, that this was how it happened, but I didn't want it to be here, and I wasn't sure how to stop it as his body pressed down on top of me. I felt him harden. My head hit the grass as his hands moved up my leg and under my skirt, and he groaned loudly, and I sucked in my breath, and his hands slipped into my underwear, and I moved my head to the side. And I felt scared, scared, scared.

Then suddenly Tessa was there, she dove in to pull me out, cradling me in her arms as she cried, dickhead get off her.

She dragged me back to her house, where I lay rocking and spewing from the bed, and she put her cool hand damp from a washcloth onto my forehead.

I wonder now if I will ever again speak with another in that distant language of giggles and chants and dark magic. I wonder if, after you lose a parent and lose your base, it is ever possible for the same city to again feel like that cross-my-heart-hope-to-die teenage secret.

26

How long do you think it would take for us to notice if Bowerbird was dead? Sami asks.

Bowerbird went camping for the weekend and it is now Tuesday. He stays at the cafe girl's house a lot now. But he still comes home regularly, as he says he is scared of her housemate. She is territorial, and he is scared to leave things in the wrong place, as she often returns it to its rightful place while giving him the look. The look is what makes me run back here, he says.

Niki says she probably would think to call someone if he didn't come home in the next two days.

But who would you call? I ask.

She pauses. I guess I only have your numbers, so you guys?

We realise we don't have each other's parents' numbers, or any emergency contacts.

My god, Niki says, my yoga studio has more information than you do.

We are silent for a moment as we think about the implications if it was one of us in trouble.

Sami says he thinks we need to buy toilet paper in bulk. I'm not pointing fingers, he says, but we are always running out, and I feel like I'm always the one buying it, and I don't want to be pissed off at you guys because of nature and all, so I just think we should buy bulk and all chip in to pay for it.

Here, I found this place, he says, showing us his laptop screen, which I believe will suit everyone's ethics and budget.

He shows us the website for a locally run company that offers to do a monthly delivery of toilet paper that is affordable, locally produced, and environmentally friendly.

You've really outdone yourself, I say.

How many is bulk? says Niki.

Well, they deliver forty-eight rolls per month.

Forty-eight! says Niki.

There was nothing smaller, he says, and it still works out cheaper, so we all agree to buy our toilet paper in bulk.

When Bowerbird does get home later that week, he tells us his phone battery died while camping, and exclaims, what happened?

We don't have much storage, so we have stacked the toilet paper along the corridor and there is a pile on the lounge-room coffee table.

Sami looks up from the newspaper he has been reading next to it and waves his hand airily and says, bulk buying. More importantly, if you were given two extra years to live, how would you spend them?

Is it two years before an apocalypse, says Bowerbird, or have I been told I'll have two years added on to the age I die, but really, I will die young at thirty-five, and so this is more of a question of how I should live my life now, and you are asking me about values and what really counts in life?

Why do men always find a way to bring things back to their apocalypse fantasies? No one mentioned the apocalypse in this scenario, says Niki, who has just arrived home from work.

I went on a Bumble date with a guy who asked what I would do if I knew a zombie apocalypse was coming, Niki says while putting down her bag. And when I said I would embrace it and eat cheese, make love and shoot myself, he said he knew a good bunker spot in Sydenham, and he would save me. I think he missed my point entirely; we clearly have little in common.

See, says Bowerbird, turns out he knew he was really asking a very deep, revealing question, and when you put it like this it seems like a good date question to sort out the riff raff and get to an essentialist sensibility. I might use it.

Next month, a new supply of toilet paper arrives and we have to store the excess rolls in laundry cupboards, kitchen cupboards, and under the stairs, so often we open doors and rolls fall on top of us. When friends come around for a drink, we sometimes give them a parting gift of a roll, which they are always grateful for, and we feel like kind benefactors dispensing all our abundance.

27

Katie and I are sitting on the grassy knoll in North Bondi mid-week on one of the last days of summer, and labradoodles and beautiful people lounge around on the beach below.

Why don't any of these people work? I ask her.

I realise we are also at the beach in the middle of the week, and we are also both currently semi-employed, but beneath our sunglasses we are both stressed about it, and somehow these people seem different, laughing with ease as though daily life is filtered Instagram light, salty ocean sprays, and mid-week brunches.

Trust-fund babies, she says, peering over her glasses.

Wouldn't it be nice, though, to just once live by the sparkling ocean this city is known for, I say.

I would love to see Sydney as a stranger, for the first time. Be like a tourist and drive down from the city and see that magical dip of the ocean, and the frangipani trees hugging the coastline, and the surfers riding the waves as smooth as oil, and think, maybe here my life could change.

Katie pushes her glasses down her nose and stares at me with a smirk.

Maybe we should move to Bondi, I suggest.

And hang out with the slashies? she asks.

Everyone in Bondi appears to be a part-time model, part-time graphic designer, part-time organic farmer at the Saturday markets.

You'd have to become my part-time lover and a part-time friend, I joke.

You'd have to start making resin jewellery, she says.

But doesn't it feel like everything could be better if we just lived in the light? I ask, convinced that the sun has magical properties.

She snorts at me and tucks her swimmers into her bum to change the course of her growing tan line.

Fuck that, she says. I think I feel like the biggest tourist here, growing up just forty minutes west, even with those English backpackers around, she says pointing to a group of fast-burning men.

I don't even feel like it's the real Australia, she says. I have no connection to this place. Punchbowl is the Australia I grew up in, but no one wants to know about that. Can you imagine the western suburbs as part of our national tourism campaign? For everyone that's just Lebs, drive-by shootings, mosques, and a place that maybe they visit for 'food safaris' so they can eat the kebabs and hummus and feel cultured, and then talk about how they love ethnic food later at some trendy city bar, and the following week vote to keep immigrants out.

This place, she says, sweeping her arm to take in the coast-line, is like some rogue Swiss state: beautiful people in an impenetrable bubble land who can afford to stay neutral in the politics of this country, because they know they will always win in life.

I don't think that's always the reason people stay neutral, I say. But I understand what you mean.

Katie and I sit in silence and watch the surfers. Those artful dodgers of the waves, Quiksilver tumbling though the white wash. One minute all goofy-limbed like puppy dogs on the shore; the next, godlike in black wetsuit armour, riding the crest of the ocean's glory.

These were the boys that captured our teenage minds.

Burning up, Tessa and I used to wait on the hot sand for the proud return of one of our crushes. Those moments split between the elements, water and earth; the separation felt mythical. In the water they transformed into salty Adonises, and I mistook their ability to read the currents of the water and the pull of the moon as insight into my own needs. Afterwards, back on land, shivering in hoodies, scoffing hot chips and tomato sauce on the sand, they pulled us girls gruffly onto their laps, and talked of post-surf war glory and strategy as if they could defeat that body of water.

In front of us three muscular men in black speedos are sitting meditating with a sign scrawled in front of them that reads, Namaste Bitches.

So aggressive, she says, laughing.

Katie is happy, I can tell. She has recently met a Brazilian guy who works at a tech start-up and runs hula-hoop workshops on the weekends. My dream guy, she says with a wink.

I watch as a long, leggy girl our age with Germanic good looks steps onto the sand. She looks born for this world of salty displays, quick reactions and speaking in 150 characters at a time, and I feel that familiar ache of wanting to trade places with her.

Baaabe, she says, and throws her arm around various people, staking her claim in swift lines as she slants her body, cocks her hip, and proves her ease with this swirling, dusted landscape.

She moves to sit against the wall, her small, tight breasts tucked into a string bikini, and her legs splayed to reveal a triangle of pastel colours. A couple of men greet her with shouts, raising their hands in high-fives, and throw their bodies across the sand and come to lie on their stomachs like sphinxes, worshipping the gentle pink and green swirls on her bathers.

You should have come to sunrise yoga this morning, Matty, she says, the hot yoga teacher was there.

People wear their bodies at the beach: flexed and primed.

They are thrown on with the same feigned indifference adopted at the front row of a fashion show; we all pretend not to notice each other's bodies. It's a performance we all play a role in, some oblivious to their part and others the subtle orchestrators of the beach ritual.

This is a city that is proud of its curves and contours, its constructed harbour and framed beauty. Yet it is not truly comfortable with the naked form. On the city beaches, semi-nudity is constantly flaunted, onlookers baited and goaded into a lasting frenzied state, but there is very little nakedness.

There are few places to view women's bodies in all their different shapes and sizes and ages and forms. Women rarely come together or abandon pretence and reveal their bodies in any collective space. The beach is the closest place to be among the exposed, but the core nudity is held onto, guarded like a secret.

I don't really want to live on this micro-city on the sand. But lately, in the share house, I have begun to feel claustrophobic. It's a house filled with restless anxiety and constant movement, as we all try to grow up and create our shape to press into this world. The wild in me is searching for a stream, an open corn field, or a mountaintop to howl from, but everywhere is concrete and people and anxiety, and I wonder why I have never noticed this before. There is nowhere to scream and a part of me understands why my neighbours just shout into their walls.

But sitting here, among the tourists and with Katie, I can see what outsiders and Europeans must feel when they arrive at this country that seems new and fresh and scrubbed clean, without a long history, and set of traditions and rules, and what possibility they must feel when they stare at that slice of blue.

Katie flips over again to even out her tan, and I think about how once you live in any place long enough, your personal history takes over and it can be hard to re-imagine those first clean moments in a landscape that is not yet tarnished by your personal myths.

28

After my morning bay run, I walk through Leichhardt where I used to come for swimming classes when I was young. My dad would take me to a woman's house, and she would throw me into the deep end of her backyard pool and see how well I could float, while my dad would sit outside and write down observations in the notebook he carried everywhere. Afterwards, my skin smelling of chlorine, he and I would walk through the leafy streets of this Italian suburb towards the cafe on the main street.

I felt like an adult as he scooped the froth from his cappuccino to spoon into my mouth. He told me this was the closest thing to a real Italian coffee shop, like the ones he used to go to in Rome many years before I was born, where the men would stand at the counter and drink their coffee in one swift gulp with just a flick of the wrist. And he would flick his wrist to show me. Flick. Gulp.

After the coffee I stood by the glazed gelato stand pretending to decide. But we always had the lemon and the pannacotta. We exulted in our small routines.

My father wolfed his down, while I was meticulous and spun it out. There is an art to gelato eating in summer under the fierce Australian sun. It is important to work from the base upwards in circular motions until a perfect conical shape is created and can be maintained. My dad watched my creation in awe—and I offered him a bite, and then watched in part-dismay and part-amusement as he bit down all squishy and ruined my perfect cone. It was part of our act.

The cafe was set up by post war migrants, and the green, white, and red awnings still flutter proudly. The staff were surly and disengaged with customers unless you told them you followed an Italian soccer team, and then their faces lit up. The place was littered with semi-aggressive signs saying, no skim, no soy, no light milk.

Once, my dad told me he bought a T-shirt in the 1970s with the name of the cafe written on it. Many years later, he wore the shirt, as a little joke, and walked in, but no one batted an eye. And this, we decided, as I took my scoop of froth, was what we liked best about the place. It didn't play favourites. It had no pretensions.

As I grew older, this became the basis for the club we formed, my dad and I: we looked for people and places that had no frills, no bullshit and preferably deadpan humour. We talked about the subtleties of British humour, and I pretended to understand political satire just so I could sit alone with him and be a part of his laughter. At family events and dinners, we caught each other's eye when a joke was too pompous, or a family member talked their children up too much, and gave each other a knowing wink.

My mother often chided him with a small slap and said he was encouraging in me what she called a waywardness.

You're filling her head, not to mention mine, with too many ideas from these lonely poets.

But I knew she wasn't really angry. And I also knew that the words of the poets contributed to their secret world of understanding.

When I walk into this cafe now, I see the menu offers skim, soy, and light milk. The staff are friendlier. They cheerily call me sweetheart and ask about my day. They have waffle cones instead of the old cardboard scratchy ones. The gelato now has fusion flavours.

But I still find my lemon and pannacotta and go sit in the sun out the front. I lick the base and create a perfect conical shape and smile. But he is not here to ruin it. The joke remains with me alone and I stare at its shape, already collapsing in the sun.

AUTUMN

29

T oday I am meeting with a librarian at a local library in Bankstown, an hour out of the city in south-western Sydney. It is reached by a warren of freeways, an inland trip from our prized coastal tropics. It is a place more known from media reports as the site of gang violence and Islamic radicalisation.

Paul couldn't make it today as his girlfriend has had a small complication and they are getting a check-up at the hospital.

Paul and I have created a list of media outlets that we want to approach, which include some traditional newspapers and some more experimental youth pop-culture magazines. Often a whole day can consist of me sending out hopeful emails enquiring if such-and-such a person could meet me for an interview. Then I send more emails to magazines pitching the story, with the name of that person, and then spend the next few days waiting to hear back.

The librarian tells me that Bankstown is not a place that evokes nostalgia or contemplation in the public mind.

The west is a distant place for many, says the librarian.

It is true, I think that Sydneysiders do not have a holistic sense of the place we inhabit. It is a segregated city and people tread their well-worn grooves and resist knowing more.

We blame the traffic. We say it is just too far away to get to the other side. We rely on the news and TV programs to tell us about our neighbours.

Sydney does not have a centre. There is no architectural

organisation around a central point and the city lacks coherence. Like an inkblot on thin paper, the city keeps expanding outwards. It is a series of enclaves, broken up by spindly passages of water that divide and conquer the city. Rivers, estuaries, and the salty brine of the ocean taint the architecture and people. Old weatherboard houses swell, sandstone facades corrode, and the newly built apartments bloat and develop mould over time from humidity and condensation.

Out west, the librarian says, there are fewer jobs, fewer general practices, less infrastructure. It's reported like it's a stain on society, she says, the place where bigots, bogans, and Lebs reign. In most minds, she says, Bankstown could be as far away as the war in Lebanon and riots in Syria—it is all an overflow of these wars anyway—viewed as a battleground for the cultural wars of others being fought down the train line.

She talks to me about the Cronulla riots, where Arab men were seen bashing Aussie surf lifesavers, and she makes air quotes and rolls her eyes. In retaliation text messages were sent out commanding, every Aussie in the Shire get down to North Cronulla to support the Leb and Wog bashing day. She tells me how Union Jack flags flew in the air as men screamed, 100 per cent Aussie Pride, southern-cross tattoos etched onto their tanned muscles. Outside of the south-west, city people shook their heads and tsked loudly from the sidelines about the 'Bogans' and the 'Lebs', and talked as if racism was a problem that only existed out in the suburbs.

She says the truth is that this area of Sydney has always evoked fear. In the 1800s, residents used to lie awake here in the black terror of the night, thinking about bushrangers. In 1826, two bushrangers from Sullivan's Gang who operated across the Blue Mountain Ranges in the Bathurst region were captured, shackled, and dragged along Liverpool Road to the present-day Bankstown water tower, where they were publicly executed, to demonstrate what happens to those thinking of embracing the romance of becoming an outsider.

She stops to tell off some school kids who have started shouting with laughter and turns back to me.

She tells me how active Bankstown was in the Second World War efforts. Many people don't realise what a big role we played, she says.

I guess areas always have secrets, she says.

I sift through the public records she hands me and think about outsiders, and if it's possible to map new perspectives on places we are born into, as I go through detailed council minutes and painstaking records of road changes, new bridges, and infrastructure.

A man named Black Charlie has an entire page dedicated to him in a local history pamphlet. His real name was Charlie Luzon, and he lived in a house of corrugated iron, near Edgar Street South. After he died, locals believed they could see his ghost haunting Marion Street.

Just a local character, the librarian says. She doesn't know why he was called Black Charlie. Some say he was Yugoslavian, or Latvian, and others say Aboriginal. He shot a rifle at 9 P.M. every night and I ask her if she knows what the ritual meant to him, if he thought he could make more sense of the world, gain more control over his life, and why the ghost of this man, about whom so little is known, invoked such a haunting.

She shrugs. I guess people have always been spooked by things they don't understand.

I collect my notes and thank her, and as I walk outside to the station past rows of orange and yellow autumnal trees, I text Paul. I pass the boys from Sierra Leone who hang out in thick clusters out the front of Bankstown station by the Lebanese cafe. One boy, decked out in all-white Adidas gear, clicks his tongue loudly and the women across the road who work at the African hair-weave shop smile and shout back.

Their hair is piled high on their heads and they sway heavily when they walk, wrapped in tight, bright, lycra prints, and laugh and bustle about the shop.

I think about Black Charlie, about bushrangers and how we decide what makes an outsider, as a kid whizzes by laughing on a scooter and almost knocks over a woman dressed in a hijab on her way to Friday morning prayers.

30

I walk into a supermarket to get some groceries for the house. They are selling trays of Easter eggs and hot cross buns and there are pictures of anthropormorphised rabbits everywhere. I see whipped cream for sale and I remember when we used to buy the cream dispensers, and the gas bulbs separately, back when high school felt like it would drag on forever.

You used to be able to buy nangs from the local supermarket before authorities figured out what kids were doing with them. The soda cream bulbs came from Franklins or Woolworths, and sometimes one of the boys would steal a carton. We wrapped them in jumpers and stuffed them into our school backpacks, because they were innocent enough not to cause direct trouble, but odd enough to create suspicion.

We had once spent a school excursion to Parliament House in our nation's cold capital ducking into corners and public toilets, sucking the gas deep into our chests and heads so our ringing bodies drowned out the noise of politicians telling us we were the future.

One Sunday afternoon we walked the back streets of the inner west after buying two-dollar vanilla ice creams at the big factory that is now a block of boutique apartments, and we sucked and slurped our way to a secret hidey-hole in a small grassy underpass by the railway tracks. The cream whip dispenser gave off a metallic clang as it fell onto the concrete and we looked around, worried. My hands were still sticky from the ice cream as I grasped the dispenser, but the rumble of trains had disguised the noise and no one had come running after us yet.

We relaxed against the gentle slope of the underpass. One of the guys pushed in the bulb like a silver bullet, and I pulled the trigger so a small hiss sounded as the gas escaped.

The guys worked in pairs. One worked as the 'loader' and set up the silver bullets in a line next to him. As the other one inhaled, it was his job to keep inserting the bulbs, one after the other, so the buzz could be maintained for as long as possible. At some point the other one dropped onto the ground, completely out of it and filled with the joyful ringing in every part of his body. I read somewhere later this activity was one of the quickest ways to lose the most brain cells.

The record at that point was twenty-eight bulbs in a row.

Next to me my friends were lying against the grass already numbed out.

We were being told more and more that our grades would affect who we would become, and we were constantly asked by teachers and parents and family friends: who did we want to become? We were looking for a way to push away the creeping reality that was slowly being built around us.

I inhaled deeply, my mouth against the dispenser.

You could hit your hand or head against any surface, nothing hurt; for those two minutes, we could cease to exist and just become a dizzy vibration, a set of cells pulsing through the air. I dropped next to them as the buzzing reverberated through our skulls and pushed into our limbs like pins and needles.

Tessa lay against the slope, moaning.

It sounds like she's having an orgasm, said one of the guys as he high-fived another.

It's true, she did. But I knew the real reason she was moaning. Time had a way of moving forwards and then backwards while you were buzzing; it felt like your atoms were breaking apart and fluttering through the air and could exist in two places at once and maybe this is what freedom—the kind that our teachers taught in history classes, or that my parents spoke about late at night, but which we could never truly feel in our bones—might actually be like.

But it was so hard to grasp, and any moment you knew that simple bodily understanding would leave you again, so that sound and moaning was the only way to anchor yourself to any trace of that feeling, before we were heaved back into the cold damp of the here and now, by the underpass, with trains rattling above.

31

B owerbird has suggested we hire a cleaner.

Sami says the very thought disgusts him.

Niki says that while the principle also disgusts her, funnily enough, the growing reality of the situation in our kitchen is starting to shift her moral compass.

Think about it, says Bowerbird. It costs eighty dollars a session, so split between four, that's only twenty each, and we could just bring them in every second week, so we are really talking about ten dollars a week for some domestic bliss.

We all agree that it is fitting that Bowerbird, who is by far the messiest and also rarely around to clean, would be the one to suggest such a thing.

Sami says it makes him uncomfortable. We are four grownups. We should be able to get a roster together and not need to pay someone else to clean up after us. What, did you never have chores growing up? Sami asks.

Sure, I had chores, says Bowerbird, but we also had a cleaner. But it's not just that. It's more that we're four people who have been thrown together, and have to sort out really personal things with each other. Like, biologically or whatever, it's more the kind of stuff we're supposed to be figuring out in a family. And maybe it's not the natural order of things to be share housing at our age. So, I just figured it would take away some of the stress of the situation for all of us.

Wait, you don't think we're a family? asks Niki.

There is a pause and Bowerbird shrugs his shoulders. He

seems tense and I wonder how much he has told the others about his sister's diagnosis and what his family is going through.

I agree, though, Niki continues. I have been feeling pretty resentful about the cluttered dishes, and just simple chores. Like, I think I am the only one who actually cleans the toilet around here, and it's not fair.

Sami says he still finds it problematic. He says, so, what, because traditional family models are breaking down and the cost of living is high, we're now somehow entitled to have a cleaner for the house? It's ridiculous. You guys are always complaining about not having enough money, but then you would just hand over a twenty because you don't want to feel awkward with each other?

Pretty much, yeah, says Bowerbird.

Sami says it is an issue of class. It doesn't sit right with him.

How are you acting high and mighty in this? asks Niki. You get other people to do basically everything else for you. You get people to drive you around in Ubers, you get others to make your food and then Deliveroo it, you get alcohol delivered to our door when you're too lazy to walk to the bottle shop, and you actually have a secretary.

The title is executive assistant, actually.

So, what makes this a class issue any more than these other services?

Or, says Bowerbird, is it just because they are available on an app, so it somehow removes the class dimension for you? Like, you'd feel uncomfortable if it were a Filipina maid, but would you be okay with getting a cleaner if it was some white undergraduate arts student we could hire via Airtasker?

Point taken, says Sami, holding up his hands. But I do think there is a key difference, yeah. It's about choice again. You just don't seem to get that there is a difference between need and choice.

Wait, says Niki, if it really was a class issue, according to your logic shouldn't we actually hire the maid?

Sami is starting to look pissed off. Look, I can't work out the full moral argument right now. I have a lot going on at work, and I don't need this here, at home. But yeah, there's something that still feels off about this.

What do you think? he says, and suddenly they are all turning to look at me.

I have been sitting at the table observing, like it's some sporting match, and I sort of forgot that I was actually in the room. I don't know what makes people so sure of things.

I shrug my shoulders, and say, oh, I don't really know, and give a small laugh.

And Sami throws up his hands exasperated. You do. You do have opinions, and you do know, he says. You can't keep hiding by sitting on the fence. Your silence is a choice too.

The comment stings me. I try to continue as if I haven't noticed his tone, but then Sami grabs a beer and practically storms out of the room.

Bowerbird laughs in half shock and says to me, whoa, you really set him off.

But I'm not in the mood. And Niki is also not in the mood. She looks at Bowerbird and says, for someone who thinks we are just strangers living together and not a family, you are acting a lot like the bratty kid. I realise he must not have told her about his sister, and I want to say something, but I am not sure what, so I let it slide.

We all trail off to bed and put the cleaner debate on hold.

The following week we hardly see each other. We have different working hours and various social obligations, but I can't help feeling like we're all avoiding each other, and the house feels under pressure.

My mum calls several times, but I let them all go to voicemail as I don't have the energy to talk to her. I think about what Sami said, about my silence being a choice. I feel judged and I think of things to say back to him to express my indignation. But maybe it comes from some nagging feeling that he is right.

The next week, the dishes are piled high, and Niki comes home and we hear something shatter on the floor followed by her scream. Sami and I come downstairs from where we have been hiding in our separate bedrooms and she asks, where the fuck is he? It's Bowerbird's week on the cleaning roster, and guess what, he isn't here again.

She glares at Sami, who puts his hands in the air and says, okay, okay, we will make the choice. And so we hire a cleaner.

32

T he Uber driver tells me he also works shifts as a train
guard.

Do you see interesting things? I ask.

Not on the good side of interesting, he replies. People act
tough. It's pretty depressing, eh? He is fidgety and has a nervous laugh.

It's a cool evening and he has picked me up on Balmain
Road from outside the hospital in Rozelle. This is a draughty
city. That's what no one ever tells you. Even Sydneysiders don't
accept it and look at the sky accusingly during the colder
months. Girls wear dresses through the wind-tunnel days and
complain. This is not part of the deal with this city.

Taylor Swift blasts out of the speakers of his shiny blue Mazda.

What were you doing in there? he asks. It's creepy.

At night, it is. It is a giant sprawling park with winding
paths and nooks and crannies. The art school is here, and it
was also formerly home to the asylum. In the daytime, it is
bright and leafy. Paths trail down to the bay where weekend
soccer games are held.

I used to come here with my high-school boyfriend. We
would go for drives to find places to make out, and push the
car seats back and clumsily move over the handbrake with lots
of thumps and swearing and panting. The car was the only
space we had that was ours and inside it felt private. But there
was also the small thrill that we could be seen any moment. He
would go down on me, my legs spread wide open to the inner

bay. Here in this car, coming and laughing, we would talk about the people we wanted to become.

He was funny. That was his persona: the comedian. The guy that everyone wanted to make a speech at their eighteenth birthday party, the guy that the school would call upon to lighten the mood at assembly, the guy that everyone looked to for entertainment. He used to like narrating what we were doing, like he was making a movie:

> She watches him cut the cheese toastie with his knife, thinking he looks just like a Greek warrior god. She rolls her eyes at his masculine defiance and punches him in the stomach, his butter knife wavering dangerously close to her hair that she just spent all her savings on getting done. Ow, she got me!

He said to me once that knowing how easy it was to make crowds laugh made him lose respect for people.

It's so formulaic, he said. Once you know what people want, and how similar we all are, it kind of makes you sick.

He kept everyone at arm's length with his jokes, and said his biggest goal was to know what it felt like to be really close with someone.

I had no idea what I wanted, but still thought the answer might be found in acting, and I was spending a lot of time in youth plays and auditioning on weekends for short films that offered 'ethnic best friend' parts. My boyfriend would circle ads for Indian, Spanish, Italian, Greek, and Lebanese roles, and hand them to me saying, see it as an advantage, Aussies can't really tell the difference, so you can get them all.

I wanted to do something that made people feel. I told him this down by the water and felt stupid saying it. I thought he would start narrating my discomfort. But instead he held my hand and said he understood, and told me it would happen, but that because I overthought everything it would take a long time.

Just watching you decide which can of tuna to buy is painful enough, so be patient in deciding what you want to do.

One night I stood in the middle of a supermarket aisle, surrounded by all the cans and all the information bubbling away in streams in my brain about which brand killed dolphins, and which brand used open harvesting, until I felt weighted with too much responsibility to decide, and was close to tears when he found me.

It was down by the water he told me he hoped one day to marry me. He said if he couldn't do that, then he wanted to have a daughter like me.

You know, just to have a daughter who has a relationship like you do with your dad. It's rare, I reckon.

It was the most beautiful thing anyone had ever said to me. Aloud, I said, that was creepy. He gave a thin, sinister smile and began his narration: And it was at this moment she realised all this time she had been dating an escaped patient from the asylum.

Almost on cue a siren sounded.

They found me! he shrieked, jumping out of the car, and we chased each other laughing, shouting, escapee, escapee, escapee.

I do writing classes here, I tell the Uber driver.

Oh yeah, how come? he asks.

I met again with the hospital grief therapist recently, and she asked me what age I felt. She told me that when people lose someone they often revert back to an age where they last felt that sense of abandonment and act out in the same way. She told me about a woman who lost her husband and began having a lot of sex with random men. She was so upset and confused by it, until she realised she was acting like she had at seventeen, when her cousin died.

Teenage years are very powerful, the therapist said. She suggested I keep a diary, perhaps like I did as a teenager. I had never written in a diary. But I understood what she was saying to me: you need to find somewhere to put your dark shapes.

And I thought about my father, sitting at his desk, scribbling and writing into the night and so, on a whim, I enrolled in these writing classes.

I'm bored, I say instead. The driver nods.

I ask him more about being a train guard. He tells me he just fell into it, but it was more training than he expected. And now it's been six years. He tells me the shifts are hard, often ten hours long and at irregular times.

The early mornings are the worst, he says. Going to work at odd hours plays games with your mind. And you see a lot of people at their worst. Like at their darkest hour, and that's hard.

I ask him what the other people he works with are like.

That's the thing. You don't talk to anyone much in this job. It's lonely. I don't even know the guy driving the train. We just go around in loops.

Coming home after being on a train all day, and driving after work. It's a long day, I say. You doing this Uber stuff because you're saving for something?

I don't really know. I mean, it's the money. I suppose the next stage in life is buying a house, even though I don't have anyone to make a home with. But there's something else—I don't know. It's not like anything I've ever done before. Time was stretching out pretty lonely for me. I like talking with people, something to make me feel connected or something . . . it stops you thinking about all the other things, you know?

He looks at me. I guess I'm bored too, he says.

We both laugh nervously and nod. The GPS dings to let us

know we're close to our destination. He hands me a bottle of water.

It's a little extra, which gets me a good rating, he says.

I say goodnight, walk into the house, and I tap the five little yellow stars into my phone.

33

The woman stands on Devonshire Street. Her face is drawn and her hisses and threats have lost their venom. Her hair is stringy and hangs down her face, curling at the end like a sad question mark. Her cardboard sign weighs down her slight frame and her arms stretch out in the shape of a crucifix to keep it balanced. On both sides of the board are blurry pictures of dead babies. She looks tired, and I almost feel sorry for her, this woman who has been a fixture of Surry Hills for as long as I can remember.

But she didn't seem so pathetic ten years ago. She had power then.

It was our final year of school and we were waiting for our exam results. It was a time of freedom, but one that we knew would draw to a close any day, so everyone sought pleasure with abandon. There were parties everywhere: at homes, at parks, on the streets. Those of us of age or with fake IDs went to the clubs in the Cross that played the obscure house music we all pretended we loved. The private-school cohort arranged to go on cruises to Nouméa and Fiji, and we made fun of them, but also felt a twinge of envy, sitting in the park with our long-neck beers and hip-hop blaring from portable speakers.

Tessa was leaving with her group of intimidating girlfriends. They were from a majority Anglo-Catholic part of Sydney and all went to one of those schools that exhibited vestiges of English boarding schools with their measured skirts and learned decorum. They spoke about 'the grounds' at school and 'French summer hols' and where to get the best spray tans before debutante ball, but even more frightening than their poise was their calculated understanding of power. Tessa said they would invite all but one of their girlfriends to slumber parties and then call the one who wasn't invited and put her sobs on speakerphone. At parties, I saw as they watched on with tight faces as boys played 'pass the parcel' with one of their friends and each guy in a circle took turns sticking a finger in her. Their eyes roved up and down her body, hardening.

She loves it, the slut, the girls said in a scripted manner as they chain-smoked in bum puffs at the back of the garden.

They were always sweet to my face. I went to a different school, was part of a different scene, and posed no threat. But I watched my words with them.

When Tessa came back from her cruise I went around one afternoon. She pulled me into her room, locking the door behind us. She was shaking.

I missed my period, she said.

Oh, I said. Does Damien know?

Tessa had been dating what could only be referred to as a man. He was six years older than us, with broad shoulders and a job, and he shaved and had an apartment, but he still hovered around the schoolgirls, laughing along with all the jokes, which made me feel odd.

Oh fuck, fuck, fuck. She pushed her fingers hard against her eye sockets. I put my arm around her.

He doesn't know, she mumbled into her chest. It might not be his.

Well, honesty is probably the best policy, I recited. It sounded static in her room.

Oh, I don't even know whose it is. It was just so wild on that cruise. Everywhere you looked people were fucking and everyone was half naked. And there was this crazy night, you know . . .

I didn't know. I listened, partly in awe and partly envious, to the stories of my friends' torrid love lives, the push-and-pull that seemed almost violent. But sitting there in Tessa's room with the curtains drawn and the sounds of her little brother thumping a football outside, I felt useless. I could see we were beginning to be a part of something real and adult and I didn't want to be here.

Damien can never know.

I nodded again, unsure if I really knew how to keep secrets.

What do you want to do? I asked, looking for her guidance in how to deal with this secret world. I felt tired. I was already exhausted by the looming consequences that would play out over the next few weeks, but I tried to make soft reassuring sounds. She looked at me, scared, but her eyes also shone with the drama.

I will have to get rid of it.

It didn't surprise me. But I knew it was different for her. She had all that Catholic guilt to deal with. She said Naomi from her school knew of a place in Surry Hills where she'd had hers done. Naomi had a car and said she would take Tessa, and I said I would come along and wait.

When the day came we parked on one of the small side streets. Tessa was wearing long baggy pants and a hoodie. Naomi looked poised and flipped out her phone every few minutes to text updates to the other girls and I wondered if we were on speakerphone as we sat in the car talking. It was late morning on a weekday, but the streets teemed with people jumping in and out of cafes and business meetings. There were a couple of homeless people huddled on front stoops and a man screaming vaguely at the streets below from the housing commission. I looked at Tessa. Her face was pinched.

We walked towards the clinic.

The stringy-haired lady was there. There were only three of

them standing out front, but it felt like an army. Cardboard posters. Chants. Those shards of words hurled at us.

Life. Death. Body. Womb. Guilt. It Has Fingernails.

Naomi walked purposefully through them, shielding Tessa. But I stopped. The lady's face was contorted with a fury that had no edges. She looked up and down my body, her eyes boring into mine. And then that word came snaking out of her mouth, the long hissing, ssssssssluts.

In the bright waiting room Tessa was signing forms and Naomi was flicking through women's magazines. I joined her. Page after slick page of women's ripe bodies, flesh bursting off the glossy paper, blurred with the metallic smell of the clinic. And I suddenly hated them all. I hated the women in the magazines and their unattainability, I hated the lady outside with her judgment, I hated Naomi with her polished pretences, and most of all I hated Tessa, for not thinking about the consequences of her body and what women can't escape.

We waited for about an hour until Tessa came out of one of the rooms, bent over, and we rushed towards her.

Are you okay? I asked.

She nodded.

We walked outside, our hands raised, bracing our faces for what lay outside, but the lady and her slogan army had left for the day.

oogle Maps keeps telling us we have arrived at our destination, but we can't see where we are supposed to enter and so we are driving in circles.

Paul is driving while I navigate.

Thank god it is getting colder, he says. His girlfriend is just over six months into her pregnancy, and he says her feet and hands were swelling up in the heat. His car has no heating and I wrap a scarf around myself and he says he really needs to splurge on some air conditioning for his poor girlfriend.

He stops the car in one of the backstreets on our third time around and takes the phone from me. He looks surprised, gives a shrug, and says, you weren't lying, it's a fucking warren.

Paul and I thought we would recognise the place immediately. We have been watching this building on the news lately, with its prefabricated stretches of nondescript grey aluminium. It is normally shot from an aerial view as inmates jump up on roofs with their mouths sewn shut, or from outside, as protesters barricade the fences with their slogans.

I just never realised it was smack-bang in the middle of people's backyards, Paul says.

It is true. It is strange to realise the country's biggest onshore processing centre stands, like Paul says, sweetly nestled on the edge of people's backyards. Some refugees and asylum seekers are locked up here indefinitely, but our view is of sprinklers, garden gnomes, and welcome mats.

We start the car up again and eventually find what looks

like an industrial driveway. The view changes, becoming a landscape of fences, security cameras, offices, and parked cars. The official entrance to the detention centre is next to warehouses for Tru Blu Beverages, Aussie Baby, and Hyalite One-Stop Hydroponic Superstore.

The car park is busy. Cars are manoeuvring in and out of the tightly painted parking lines and broken bits of Farsi and Tamil and Urdu tumble over the sound of engines and radios. I recognise loose clumps of the words from my childhood. But the tone here is different. The accents are thicker and the people are distressed and I can't understand the words in this context.

Inside the visitor centre, families and friends are being questioned and subjected to screening processes. Paul and I join one of the untidy queues, and one of the officials looks overwhelmed, and she keeps asking us to form orderly lines. But people are upset and confused and stand in stunned formations, and I think of the way everyone jostles in India, and how I would laugh with my mum as two-lane traffic magically became four lanes of weaving and honking.

The look on the woman's face becomes harsher as she doesn't understand this. She seems to take it as a personal insult to her authority and she snaps at people. When Paul and I finally get to the front of the queue we are turned away.

Visiting hours are now over, the woman barks at us and others, fed up.

We drive back out to the entrance of the complex to take some photographs from the street and within a few minutes a security van pulls over and demands we delete the images.

What a shitshow, mutters Paul.

We are not sure what to do. We have already talked to other people in the community, who were once locked up in the detention centre. But many of them signed forms promising not to speak about their time in the centre, and they are too afraid they will be sent back to risk speaking publicly.

We drive to one of the side streets to plan our next move. On one side are whitewashed houses and manicured lawns and on the other side are the outlines of the security fence.

We walk around the block, peering past people's houses to their lawns broken off by the bordering barbed wire fences, which have a military look to them.

We walk past an elderly couple sitting on their front porch in plastic chairs, tenderly holding hands. Behind them is a full panoramic view of the detention centre. They wave to us and ask what we are looking for and we tell them we are doing a story about Villawood.

Nina introduces herself and says this is her husband, Mihajlo, or Michael we might say, and he nods his head. They tell us they are from Serbia and have lived in this house for twenty-three years. She says living here has always been peaceful and quiet and that it is a perfect place to raise a family. Michael says he loves the sense of community they have created with neighbours from places as far away as Iraq and Vietnam. And they smile at each other.

They invite us inside for a cup of tea and say that if we want we can look at their backyard. In the kitchen, their daughter is bustling around making sandwiches. She looks up from slicing bread, and exclaims something in Serbian, and Nina waves her hand and says something back, and she gestures for us to walk out the back screen door. Outside is a clothesline with their whites hanging and more of the garden gnomes. Their grandson, who must be about four, is busy kicking his bouncy ball against the fence the family currently share with the locked-up refugees and asylum seekers.

Michael tells us this land near the detention centre was cheaper than surrounding suburbs. The government made a deal a long time ago, that they would make this affordable housing. It's funny, he says, because when they first moved here, that place, and he points across the fence, was never made to lock people up. It was set up to house migrants arriving after the war when this country brought us over to do labour work.

Did you know, Nina and I lived in there for one week, when we first arrived in this country. We were free to come and go. And when they told us this house was going cheap, we bought it, because we liked the area. We never imagined our first home would become a prison.

Nina says no one ever tells them what's actually happening in the centre.

We are told these people are illegal. They have not followed the rules or something and so they must stay there. I don't know if I really understand it all. Mihajlo? Remember that time? Nina looks at Michael, and he nods.

The kids in there, she says, turning to us, they used to play on the field, and we had this same fence, but it looked different then, more like a friendly fence. And we didn't know anything then about what was happening, and we just heard these kids playing. And so, I took some chocolate down.

Remember? She looks at Michael again and he nods again.

The little kids' hands came through the fence and grabbed the chocolate and I didn't know what they were saying, something in Arabic maybe, but it didn't matter, we just made sounds through the fence and we were laughing. And then this guard came and he moved the children. And later they came to the house and told us not to have contact with them. I said, bah, it is just chocolate, and they are just kids, remember I said that, Mihajlo? And they said no, they said something like they are prisoners or some word. And that we shouldn't talk to them anymore. And then maybe two months later, this new fence went up.

There is a saying in Serbia, Michael says, that a good neighbour is like having a brother. I have heard some stories. Some of those people in there try to kill themselves. You don't treat your neighbour like this. We lived there for one week. Nina and I, inside this same place.

Their grandson trips over and starts to cry. Michael picks him up and Nina pats his arm.

We try not to think about it much, she says. But it's funny because sometimes Mihajlo and I say we feel like maybe now we are in a prison with all this barbed wire and fences around us. It can be hard to know who is on the inside and who is on the outside sometimes.

Their grandson squirms in Michael's arms. He feels better and wants to be put on the ground again. Michael laughs and says, easy, easy, and the moment he places the boy down on the grass he is off running to pick up the bouncy ball lying at the foot of the fence.

35

I met Aleks in an art history class, in our second year at university. We were both doing it as an elective, thinking it would be easy. We went on a date to the Art Gallery of NSW and he asked who my favourite landscape painter was.

I said, I hate landscapes. At least, I hated Australian landscapes.

I said to him, I don't like the way that nothing feels at stake.

I was nervous as I said this. He made me nervous. Worse, he made my centre shake, and I felt like I had to state bold things, or he would fill up my pauses and I would lose whatever space I had created for myself. He moved through rooms at strident angles, cutting air and distance at once, and I had to trot to keep up.

The first rooms of the gallery are dedicated to early colonial landscapes and filled with gifted paintings and generous bequests from familiar-sounding families. Bored women dressed up in English finery waiting at lone sheep stations, shearers, muscle and wool. Horse-drawn carts across frontier settlements. There was something uneasy for me in the way the Australian bush and identity sat in these galleries. English culture superimposed over harsh bushlands and bordered with heavy gold frames. I thought about the scene in Roald Dahl's *The Witches*, where the people become trapped in the landscape paintings and spend their entire life in one scene aging among the rowboats and the geese, and I shuddered at the thought of being caught in one of these early Australian scenes.

In the classical realism room were rows of Australian works emulating the Greeks. These rooms were filled with artists who went abroad to schools in Paris and London and came back to render the Australian psyche with their learned techniques and materials. But they still had little to do with our specific type of heat, or island loneliness, or the crack-your-heart-open bush-land.

We went across to see the main exhibition on loan, the oily Caravaggios, where my knees weakened, and I quietly wished for the same thud of recognition in the pit of my stomach for the Australian works. We came out the other end to the tea-room filled with the light and air and bright sun reflecting off the water below that had nothing to do with the dark European moods. As if sensing my own brewing mood, he grabbed my hand and said, let me show you something.

He took me across the foyer into another room, where I saw Fred Williams for the first time. All the lonely brushstrokes burning up on the vivid desert. A landscape without sentiment or story but it captured the shape of an emotion. In another room hung Djan'kawu Creation Story, painted with real mate-rials—bark, ochre, and the clay and colours that I see each day in this country. Aleks told me that Indigenous paintings weren't even allowed to be hung as art in galleries until recently. He showed me Brett Whiteley, the quick flurry of the Harbour Bridge strokes, and in another, a pale pink bird swerving across the sky, and everywhere, blue. He whispered in my ear how this piece always turned him on, that sensual tilt of the harbour filled with all its longing.

And as he looked at the painting, I saw the landscape of our next six years flash before us: the urgent desire as we would suck the marrow from each other's bones, living so high and light, the fights through the pitted Sydney streets at night, and the moment he would eventually leave me. But I also saw just how much would be at stake, and I chose this landscape.

36

S ami has convinced me to sell my bicycle. It is not good
for me hold on to signs of 'him', he says delicately.

Sami says that the things we use each day need to be
clean—our clothes, what we use to decorate our room, the
bike—everything should be imprinted with our present and
not our past because these inform our mental state. This makes
sense but it terrifies me. I am a keeper of things. A nostalgia
hoarder. I drag suitcases from house to house of trinkets
picked up on travels. I have kept all the letters ever written to
me.

But I decide to be open to his suggestion. Sami touches my
arm and suggests that perhaps I am having trouble letting go
of much more than just my past relationship, but I give him a
look, and he withdraws his hand, and instead he sits with me
patiently while I set up an ad on Gumtree.

I click on To Sell from the drop-down menu and enter the
bicycle's name, Betty. Sami reaches across and hits delete. No
personal details. No stories. No projecting. Keep it clean, he
says.

I enter the bike's make and design and colour. Powder blue.

And I remember when I came into the store to get the seat
adjusted and the bike man said, oh, you are the lucky lady who
got this bike. Your man is just one of the sweetest I've seen.
The colour. When he came in here, he was so worried about
the colour. He sat on each bike seat to try to imagine how each
one would feel for you. It was strange and touching watching

this man thoughtfully sit on all these ladies' bikes. I laughed and said I could see it all.

Keep going, Sami says. Cullings are important, he says.

We get through the list of information and Sami picks a little picture of me to insert into the owner details. A smiling one so they don't think you're a psycho, he says, and we click submit.

There. How do you feel?

And all I can think about is how Aleks used to pack little sandwiches for us to take on bike trips and they were quite terrible, the sandwiches, filled with strange fillings that weren't very fresh, but he would always cut them in triangles, and this always broke my heart.

But Sami looks so happy, and he has been sweet to sit here on this Sunday afternoon making an ad with me, and I am happy we are getting along again, so I give him a smile and shake my shoulders and say, great, I feel just great.

The next day I get a little mail icon and a girl says she is interested in the bike, and I tell her she can come over in the afternoon and when she arrives and sees it, she squeals. But it is so cute! I love it! And the basket!

I smile at her and I remember when I was in Aleks's backyard. I lay sprawled on the trampoline kicking my feet in the air as he sat alongside me making me this basket, and we had this song we liked to sing together, so we hummed this, as he occasionally reached over to gently bite one of my wriggling feet.

The girl has just moved to Sydney to be with her boyfriend, and she doesn't know many people, and it is hard because he has a whole world here, and sometimes she feels like she is a burden, because she just feels so dependent on him for every part of her mood, and that she is not normally like this, and that perhaps having a bike will give her some feeling of autonomy. It is quite hard to make new friends, she says, and she can't tell if it is her age, or this city, or her personality. Whenever she makes connections with people, they tell her that they should hang out sometime, but that sometime never seems to arrive.

I ask her how long they have been together and she says, just one year, so this is the make-or-break stage.

She asks me why I am getting rid of this bike, it is so sweet. And I tell her that my ex-boyfriend gave it to me and that we are no longer together. She looks sad. I am worried that I have made her think of her future with her boyfriend, and so I say quickly that I was very happy with him when I had this bike, and that he was a kind person. And that I was mostly laughing when I rode this bike. And I mean it. I just don't mention any of the things that happened to us later.

Her face looks renewed, and she smiles, and says again, almost in a reverent whisper, it is such a sweet bike.

She hands over the cash and as she mounts it my heart drops right down and I immediately want to reach out and take the bike back, but it also soars as I see her wobble and then find a steady rhythm as she rides down our little street to her new life in this city.

37

Niki says she thinks one of the hip-hop guys who lives in the house near us is cute. She also thinks he's a cokehead. And she's conflicted.

It is a Sunday and we are doing a deep clean of the kitchen cupboards as we have discovered we have weevils. We Googled what to do, and are now going through every item in the cupboard, wiping down every opened package and cleaning every Tupperware container.

Niki and I got stuck with the job because of our timetables, but we have negotiated with Bowerbird and Sami, and in return they have said they will cook for us this week.

I say the hip-hop guy would probably never date her.

She looks aghast. Why?

Well, I think he's a bit racist. So there's another conflict for you.

We are both wearing rubber washing-up gloves. I am sitting on the floor with a sponge for wiping while she is standing on a stool and passing the containers down to me.

She snorts, that guy, who is mostly high and passed out or beatboxing about girls? Is it because he listens to Eminem sometimes? Not all misogynists are racists, you know. Remember my ex, Damo?

One of Niki's boyfriends from back in her modelling days owned some construction sites and was some kind of C-list celebrity and he used to take her out on yachts and to fancy bars. He expected women to dress a certain way and was constantly talking about 'family values' and 'family men' while he snorted lines off young girls' backs.

Well, his music choices alone should be enough for you to not want to date him.

I didn't say I wanted to date him. I just said I think he's cute. In this kind of grotesque or unlikely way. You know when there's something a little off about them, and it's kind of intriguing and attractive?

It's okay, we often become attracted to our oppressors at some point.

She hits me and then squeals at a flutter of wings as she opens a jar. This is so gross. And she points to the small white larvae clinging to the corners of the jar and we both gag a little.

I fill the sink with hot water and squirt in wild amounts of detergent and finally say, that whole house has underlying white pride.

Okay, fine, I'll bite. Like what?

Well, I say holding up my fingers to count my points, they fly the Australian flag. I mean. We know what country we're in.

Personally, I appreciate the friendly reminder, says Niki, and she drops a load of infested Tupperware into the sink.

The lyrics to their songs say things about Aussie pride, screwing women over, and how nothing and no one is ever going to change them. Ever. You get my drift?

Not really . . .

Fear of change is classic nationalistic behaviour. The power structures will remain, and no foreigners, or women, or revisionist history, are ever going to change that.

You're pretty bad at adapting to change. You got all upset when Sami made you sell that bike. Does that make you a nationalist?

The other day, I say, ignoring her and holding up my third gloved finger, when he was talking to you, he said, I'm not racist but . . . and then said a whole bunch of shit about all the immigrants in this area. And, I might add, you laughed. I saw you.

Niki throws her hands up, sprung, it's true and I'm not proud, but impersonations always make me laugh, you know that.

Wait, I say, somehow I'm doing all the cleaning of the actual weevils. We need to swap roles.

Fine, I thought I could distract you with this rant, says Niki. Okay, what else have you got?

Well, all the girls they date are blonde, or at least they're definitely white.

Yes, they have a type, this is true. But you know your friend Andy, he pretty much only dates Asian women, what does that make him then?

Mmm, true, I respond. Oh, and, and, I say, getting excited, the only time I've ever seen anyone awake in that house during the daytime was the morning they were coming back from the Anzac Day dawn service. Dawn service. Think about it.

That's patriotism! That's different! They went to support the diggers.

Oh, c'mon, what people in our generation do you know who are genuine patriots?

That's a very good point, we don't believe in anything, she says, laughing. But I'm still not buying this. I can't even tell now if you are joking or if you believe this. What you just listed is how half this country acts, or at least half the guys. What are you trying to say?

I shrug my shoulders. Maybe it's not his fault. I mean, is it that surprising that a country built on white-supremacist values has, well, some white-supremacist values?

Jesus, okay, I think you're taking it too far, I won't date the hip-hop guy.

I knew it, I say, wiping down the countertop, I knew you wanted to date him.

Niki doesn't respond.

We keep scrubbing for the rest of the afternoon in silence as we check every nook and cranny for tell-tale signs of weevils hiding between the cracks.

38

In the morning at a cafe, I read an article that says in some parts of the United States shoes are thrown over electricity lines as a sign of celebrating graduation. In other states it marks the spot of a gang member's death. The same article says that in Australia, the dangling sneakers mean someone had lost their virginity.

That's not true. Where I grew up, at least, it was supposed to mean a place you could buy drugs.

This was the information passed down from friends' older brothers, partly to impress us, and partly because no one really knew, and as kids we would walk the past the flying Nikes, Reeboks, and Cons and point and snicker and make bold claims about what we would buy from there when we were older.

I went around to Tessa's place one afternoon and she showed me three little green pills nestled in the palm of her hand. Ecstasy, she said. She snorted when I asked her if she'd got them from that intersection at Parramatta Road and she told me they'd bought them off one of the boys dating Naomi. I felt stupid. Old shoes and power lines had nothing to do with our suburban middle-class world.

When I saw the pills, I thought of Anna Wood's death splashed over the newspapers, and parents freaking out about party drugs and underage raves. The phrase 'such a waste of youth' was repeated in hushed whispers by adults on the phone, and although we were still too young to understand the full meaning, their fear was infectious. I could never remember if the problem was that she forgot to drink water and got too dehydrated, or that she drank so much that her stomach exploded.

Tessa asked again if I wanted to come down the park with them this time and even though I didn't want to take those little green pills, I was curious to see what this wasted youth looked like, so I said yes.

We met up with some boys who we didn't know very well. When we arrived, some of the guys had already taken their pills. They had brought their speakers, and were swaying and laughing crazily under a tree.

That was the first time I met Andy, and he stood in the middle of the group, already peaking, his clean blond hair flopping as he rapped along passionately to lyrics about killing black people with Dr. Dre as if he knew anything about this world of violence or struggle. He had big green eyes, and pretty girls hovered around him. Naomi and another girl from Tessa's school sat with their legs awkwardly tucked underneath them, and rolled their eyes and laughed with suspicious faces at the boys' easy banter. Then the girls all looked at each other excited and held their little pills between their thumbs and their forefingers and counted to three before they put them in their mouths.

And then they waited while I lay back and watched.

Nothing happened for a while. I got bored and went over to the playground and pushed the swings around distractedly. When I came back Naomi was laughing hysterically and pounding the ground. But soon the laughter turned into tears, and her eyes popped in terror. She started running around the park madly, like she was trying to run away from herself. Her friend started screaming and saying we should call her boyfriend, while Naomi kept saying, no, no, he will be so mad I did it without him, he can never know. Some of the boys went running after her, swift shapes cutting through the darkness, disrupting the still of the park. They crash-tackled her and Andy carried her over his shoulder, making soothing sounds while she thrashed about wildly. I moved to give her some water, and then couldn't remember if that would make her stomach explode, so I hovered around uselessly with a bottle.

They stood in a circle around her, holding her hands and chanting, it's a good pill, it's a good pill, over and over, until I saw her muscles slowly relax and her eyes roll back to a place of belonging.

It was the beginning, before Naomi would talk as if she had done drugs her whole life, and bum puff joints and act aloof and bored when people asked her what it felt like.

It was the beginning, before Andy's mum died and he would go on to snort and sniff and swallow his way through his twenties.

It was before Tessa would leave the country to pursue acting, recreating her secret worlds on the screen. Her broken relationships were splashed across the tabloid magazines, and in the pictures, her eyes shone with the same look of drama as they had, years ago, at the clinic. I would see her every few years, and there would be some story of glamorised pain, and although we would remain in each other's lives, something became clear this night for me, about the different ways we would go in life.

But for that moment, before things changed for all of us, Tessa and Andy and I just lay on the grass, holding hands and staring up at the power lines that crisscrossed the city and spliced the horizon. Above us, a fruit bat lay stuck on the power lines, its furry torso hanging limp, a reminder of the invisible electric current that is always charging through the city while most of us are asleep.

39

Niki tells me she keeps dreaming her teeth are falling out.

We have been to dinner and are now walking past the social housing and workers flats that sit rumble-tumble proud on High Street, Millers Point, and passersby can't look away from the chalk protests on the footpath:

Are we a society or a developer's wet dream?

The wealthy of Walsh Bay say, let our neighbours stay.

Niki says in the dreams her teeth crumble into her hands and when she runs her tongue over her gums she can feel these vestigial, knobby lumps.

What does it mean? she asks. It's creeping me out.

I tell her that listening to other people's dreams has been proven to be more distressing than visiting the dentist. She hits me.

This area was once slums, where the wharf workers lived, and then in the 1980s they turned it into public housing. The houses have one of the most prized views in Sydney, over the harbour, but now, because of the Barangaroo casino developments, the tenants are being asked to move on to make way for the new face of Sydney. Niki says it makes her sad that people seem more concerned about how this city looks than how this city feels.

This is a beloved home, one house declares.

What have we become? says another.

We board the train and pass stations where some crucial

foundation is always being excavated and reimagined. Giant cranes swing across the million-dollar skylines. Jackhammers accompany the work commute. Scaffolding and tarpaulins cloak the CBD like some Christo work. Walls are knocked down to re-envision warehouses in Alexandria.

It feels busy and purposeful, like it's part of a bigger plan. Change is progress, they tell us. Building contractors swing from ropes and tumble out of demolition sites, conquering the unsuspecting city with their authority and easy camaraderie.

Sometimes I watch the trail of high-vis vests scurry between the spaces in building zones, as everyone rushes past them, and think with awe that they are the only ones who can feel how brittle this city really is.

On the weekend my grandmother tells me that she dreams of the jasmine attar from her home in India. The women in our family wear the broody scent and it mingles with the salt-whipped breeze of the Sydney coastline. At her place on the North Shore, the mustard seeds pop and turmeric stains the faux-marble countertop as she explains to me how the family of kookaburras has been growing in confidence and is now attacking the wisteria on her balcony. She tells me she still dreams of her childhood home and that flowery smell, but now everyone is so scattered across the globe that that she can never dream of living there again. It belonged to a different time, she says.

The real-estate section in the weekend newspaper shows pictures of eager first-home buyers lined up for house inspections on the same cracked pavement near our house where the Indigenous protesters are now camping. The captions read 'Tahlia and Matt eager to buy their dream home.'

In the mornings I often pass the protest camp en route to the train station for work, smiling, head bowed, unsure. Reporters roam up and down the site. The banners scream: If you don't let us live like Aboriginals then what use is democracy?

Niki and I walk back home from Redfern station. The painting on the wall across from Redfern station is in earthy colours and reads: 40,000 years is a long time. 40,000 years still on my mind.

We walk through the concrete park that has been reinvigorated with plants and stylishly exposed beams, and I can smell the eucalyptus and the protesters' campfire.

The park slopes downward so when you're standing at the top it reveals the skyline of the city centre. Centrepoint Tower juts above the office buildings that bathe in their squares of light, while a wall painted with the Aboriginal flag sits brightly in front of us. Thunderstorms have been predicted for later tonight, and we both squeal as we feel the heavy drops that signal the beginning of a downpour.

Kids run around barefoot and excited, and we watch as the protesters run to zip up their tents and unfurl the tarpaulin. We listen to their shouts and giggles, and then there is a loud slushing sound as a puddle of water from the tarp is tipped onto the ground and drenches everyone.

Once, after he became ill, my father told me that his nights had become quieter. He would lie awake listening to the rain drum on the roof. I asked him if he thought it meant he was at peace with the idea of death.

No, he said. I don't feel this is my time. But I can't sleep. And I just can't dream the way I used to.

40

I walk across Hyde Park on my way to an interview. I swerve away from the jacked-up enthusiasm of the clip- board-wielding charity workers. I hiss at a group of ibis stalking the litter and staring down sandwich wrappers. Members of the Falun Dafa meditation crew are handing out pamphlets. Several Chinese couples are taking wedding photos by the fountain.

Twenty months ago, I met my dad near here for lunch at a place he loved, the Hellenic Club, across from the park. His appetite had not been good, but he hated feeling like he was missing out on things: he was always asking me what was hap- pening in the city and he refused to let medical appointments alter his routine or what he ate. In fact, the only concession he made to his cancer was his preference for lunch dates instead of dinner.

We walked up Elizabeth Street to a little doorway and wan- dered up the creaky stairs. There was a musty smell. Growing up, I was always taken to restaurants that were popular in his youth. Let's go to the Spanish Quarter, it was a real buzz back in the day, he'd say, or, the Royal George was the place to be for lefties. He always made plans based on a memory. This is the best bush- walking track in Ku-ring-gai; let's take the old Atherton Tablelands Rail Trail up to Queensland. And then he would always be surprised and somewhat melancholy when the land- marks were no longer there, or when the restaurant was empty.

It didn't surprise me at all. Memories cannot be relied

upon—why would these old things still be around? The city I grew up in was elastic and belonged to me and my friends as we stretched it through the nights. We knew its contours, and when something new arrived we were the first to be a part of it. Everything was powder pink and bendy and shiny for us. We hadn't had time to build a lasting memory around some fixture and then watch time fall away from under us.

The phrase 'remember when . . . ' did not yet have a place in our conversations.

I played along as we walked up yet another flight of stairs, but I also knew that we'd probably find it was now a lawyer's office, and we would end up eating at a sushi train while he grumbled about how nothing is where it used to be. So I was surprised to get to the top and be greeted by an old Greek man with impeccable manners, who seemed to recognise my dad as he ushered us over to a table with white linen cloth and told us about the whitebait special.

This is the real Greek food, my dad said. This is where I used to meet with my friends, back in the day. And this is where the politicians used to make deals, he said, and he and the waiter winked at each other.

We ordered tzatziki and a serve of spanakopita with dill sprinkled on top, and my dad talked, and was animated in a way he hadn't been for a while. This was a real institution. Malcolm Fraser, Gough Whitlam, and Paul Keating, and the trade unions, and working-class pride. He was in his element, and for the rest of the lunch he told me about what he called the 'real things' in this city, and what deals he thought were made at the table we were sitting at. He kept convincing me to order more, but I noticed he hardly touched the food himself.

I just kept eating, clots of taramosalata, and saganaki drizzled with oil and honey, and I felt my belly swell under my dress, but I kept eating in some attempt to play along and prove to him that nothing in this city was changing.

WINTER

41

Winter begins and it rains the entire month of June. I go on a first date, and we binge watch foreign movies as part of the Sydney Film Festival at the State Theatre. The wet outside feels grand against the gold facade, and inside the cinema we get to know the way the other leans forward when excited, or shuffles with anticipation in the gloom. I don't tell him this is the first time I have dated in so long, and instead we watch as people talk in dark sentences and roam the Russian tundra.

In between movie sessions we pull on our coats and scarves and walk down to Chinatown to eat steaming chicken and leek dumplings and drink jasmine tea. We pass by the carved Chinese animals atop the northern gates, and he says they were set up by feng shui experts to ward off local gossip.

I tell him I am seeing the Chinese herbalist who asks me to swallow dozens of tiny round black pills each morning, noon, and night. He asks if it is helping. I shrug. I have been waking in the night with stabbing pins and needles and nightmares. The acupuncturist told me last time that the blood is struggling to flow through my limbs because my heart is blocked.

We talk about acupuncture and the spatial arrangement of furniture as we walk past the yum cha houses with their tanks of desperate-looking fish and lobsters slowly crawling on top of each other. We talk shyly about the movies at first, but as the days of the festival progress we become experts at sizing up the moral dilemma each character faces. He deftly waves chopsticks filled with bok choy as he makes his point.

Inside the cinema, our bodies move closer, touching softly, amid the smell of popcorn and burnt butter. We snuggle into the interior world, watching other people make disasters of their lives. At one point, he asks if it is weird to only watch movies on each date, and says that I must be getting the impression he doesn't want to hear about my life. I say, it suits me well, and check my phone to see when the next one is starting. I don't tell him my father died, and we watch as a family humorously reunites on the Amalfi coast.

Afterwards, he whispers in my ear that he wants to take me home, and it has been so long, so long since I have felt anything in my body but those pins and needles, so I say yes.

We buy a bottle of red wine and throw our bodies across his polished floorboards as the rain smacks down. He tells me my neck is long, like a violin's, and that he has wanted to kiss it since the day we first met at a friend's birthday dinner. Our hands trace the outlines of each other. And then, in a whisper, he says, you have a wall around you.

His voice rises at the end like an intimate question mark as he waits, inviting me into a confessional drawing together of our worlds.

I feel a familiar punching sensation in my stomach. I don't want to lie in bed and share stories like I used to with men. I just want to sit in the dark and watch movies, with the steady breath of someone else rising and falling beside me.

The next morning, we quietly poach eggs on his stove. He sprinkles in vinegar while I make us cups of thick, black coffee. We hardly touch, separate in our own orbits of thought.

When we walk outside, the rain has stopped, the month has ended, and there are no more movies to watch.

42

One-on-one time, he called it.

He told me constantly as I was growing up how important it is. He set up times with me, even when I was younger and we lived in the same house, and these were unbreakable dates. When I was older, he took me out to dinner at restaurants with candles on the table, a bottle of red wine tucked under his arm.

He had been a bachelor until his forties and he still maintained the habit of eating out. Domesticity felt clumsy in his hands, which my mother made up for with her rich curries. His repertoire included boiled rice, boiled eggs, boiled vegetables, and then, plucked obscurely from his travels, Imam Bayildi, the Turkish Emperor's eggplant dish.

When I reached my twenties, something shifted. We would go out, and the waiters would stare. The staff would cautiously ask if he and his Miss would like the chef's special, or allude to romance in a way that made us both inwardly cringe. We didn't look alike, and people couldn't place the older white man with his young, browner daughter.

So, he often dropped in the comment early that he was taking his daughter out, or made some passing remark about his daughter's accomplishment in finishing university, and I would feel strange and embarrassed for him and for myself, and it threatened something imprecise that we had built up together. Fathers and daughters are in a delicate world that is not built strong enough to withstand questions.

Over these dinners, he told me about the Italian poet he loved, Pavese, and the time he visited the poet's city of Turin, and how Pavese was arrested for not joining the Fascist army, and just how much he admired this man and his words.

My father told me we read history and we read poetry sometimes for the same reasons. It helps us look at what we have come out of and what we are heading towards.

He said it can help us with the big questions. What it is to love, what we have destroyed and how to deal with loss.

Only now have these dinners started to feel like rare magical acts.

43

K atie and I run up the ramp and almost trip in our excitement to climb into the small Ferris wheel cabin. I fumble with my wallet as the young ticket collector comes by and she laughs and says, my shout.

It has been thundering all day, and although it has subsided to a steady drizzle by evening, Darling Harbour is almost deserted. It is the last official week of Vivid, a festival of lights that runs over winter and takes over the major harbour fronts and makes it hard to move around the city.

Signs are plastered everywhere: Your City in a New Light.

Katie's relationship with the Brazilian ended a few weeks ago. He received a job offer in another country, and Katie says that while they hadn't been together long enough to contemplate a long-distance relationship, it had also been enough time for her to feel heartbreak.

Since then she's been working at a food charity. She says she enjoys the peeling and the chopping, and working with her hands again. But she tells me she might have to stop.

It's the people, she says. I can't handle it.

The homeless people?

No, the workers. This work attracts other broken people. And I can feel we're all doing it to feel better about ourselves, which is fine, but it's attracting all this sadness, and I can't bear talking with them and feeling it. I walk into the room and I feel all their need. Like attracts like.

Tonight, because of the weather, it feels like we have the

harbour to ourselves except for an Asian couple making out in the bottom cabin. Speakers blast Frank Ocean, and green and gold laser beams dance across the dark water just for us.

I used to come to Darling Harbour in my late teens for Bacardi Latin Festival, so I could dance with the salsa instructors. Aussie guys my age held girls with limp arms, and I wanted to know what it felt like to really dance with someone from somewhere else.

One time there was an old Argentinian man who pulled me right against him, but he danced so well and it felt innocent and grandfatherly so all night we twirled close with each other. As a joke my friend gave him my number at the end of the night, but over the next few days I started getting calls that began with heavy breathing, and he would talk about his pacemaker breaking, and then his language would get filthier, and eventually I had to change my number.

Remember the place around here you could sneak in and get spirits on a Friday night for like two dollars fifty? Katie asks me. I mean, they were watered down so it probably wasn't much of a bargain. But still, those were fun. That bar is now part of a hotel and the drinks are so expensive!

Yeah, I say. And the next day I would be in such a poor way, I'd spend it watching DVDs from the new release section at Blockbuster.

Oh, says Katie, RIP Blockbuster! God, those video stores were my life for twenty years.

It's like you only come to the harbour when you're a teen and first start drinking with a hipflask hidden in your bag, and then again when you're old and don't know the good places to go anymore, she says.

Are. We. Old? I ask.

Katie rocks the cabin in protest. She says we can't be old, because we have achieved none of the things that we should have by our age: no marriage, no property, no steady income, no babies, and no assets. I mean, I wouldn't trust you with a home loan.

Thanks, I say.

We are up the top now and the wheel has stopped turning. It is high. The whole harbour glistens below us; the light bursts from the restaurants and nightclubs and the rain angles softly through the bars of the cabin. The droplets remind me of a time I was with my father in his last months, and we saw a Saint Andrew's Cross spider stretched out and suspended across the footpath outside our house. It had been raining like this the night before, and the drops still clung to the web so it shimmered in the air like an expensive diamond necklace. I told him to duck and he bent down but his head touched the web and it trembled sending the spider to retreat into its curled leaf.

We watched it for some time.

You and your mother always get me to stop and look at how these small things are changing around me, he said. I don't think I've ever had so much time to do it before. I wish I had realised it sooner, he said.

Below the Ferris wheel, the wind is pushing the water into wide, flat shapes.

It is just such a beautiful city, Katie says.

It is beautiful, I say. But it looks fake. And I hate it so much sometimes.

Katie looks at me.

It's not the city's fault, I say, it's just that there is too much here. I feel crushed. I can't breathe with all these memories everywhere.

And then I feel my shoulders start to shake. The Ferris wheel shudders with me as I begin to cry.

It's okay, she says, and holds my hand. We look at the lone figures huddled under umbrellas beneath us, who look so small and fragile next to the vast man-made harbour.

We are getting older, I say, and no one talks to you about what that really means.

She looks at me and says, with a small laugh, those Buzzfeed lists are bullshit, and she gives my hand a squeeze.

The cabin spins as the Ferris wheel moves us gently towards the ground.

The truth about getting older, she says, is you just spend more time watching the same streets and missing people that used to be in them with you.

44

Eighteen months ago, I went to a park in the middle of the city with some friends for a demonstration. It was raining, so I brought an umbrella, almost as tall as me, that someone had once stolen from Bunnings. We'd packed beers and someone had a waterproof speaker, and Andy had made a sign on green cardboard saying, Our Climate, Our Future, but the rain had got to it, so Our Future was crying.

My father had called me the night before and said he didn't know anyone his age that was going, and asked if he could join us. He had started his chemotherapy and was becoming weaker. He said he knew it was a demonstration especially for the young people, but that he had been young once, and that I am young now, and he would like to come.

I saw him waiting patiently beneath a tree on the edge of the park as it filled with groups of young people. He had forgotten to bring an umbrella, so we shared mine as we waited for the talks on the stage to begin. There was an energy in the air as a whole park of people waited for something to happen. Banners for Greenpeace, the Greens, and the United Nations jostled with homemade signs.

My dad chatted with some of my friends and grabbed a beer, but it was loud and wet, so we mainly stood around in clumps not talking, sometimes joining the rally cries. Drops from the umbrella trickled down and rolled under the collar of my jumper and my dad brushed more of them away and we laughed.

And I remember the feel of those cool drops and his hand lightly against me, and the electricity of this moment we shared together.

But we were also trying, in our own confused way, to say this bigger thing that none of us can truly comprehend, which is that time is running out.

And that beneath the surface, time was running out for him and for me, and for all of us, and here in this rainy park we were upset because we were slowly understanding that we were on the verge of losing everything.

45.

Not long after the rally, my father stayed in a nursing home for ten days. More and more he needed the kind of care that was difficult for us to provide.

Respite care, he told me, savouring those words and their suggestion of rest. It was a nice place, as far as these places go. It was an old converted house in Petersham on a leafy street. They only took up to twelve residents. I joked and said he was going back to his communal socialist roots. They would eat their meals together around the kitchen table, and there was a living room with a fireplace. But all the windows had bars. The light was white and sterile. They had to ask permission to leave, so the nurses knew their comings and goings. It smelled like disinfectant.

I arrived one evening in time for dinner. My dad asked if it was okay if his daughter had some of the dessert, and the nurse smiled at me.

I sat at the table with them. They had eaten a simple meal of spaghetti and vanilla custard. Everyone was here for a different reason. Fernanda told me she came from the land of Venetian glass. Her grey hair was in an elegant chignon and her face was framed by glass earrings. She liked to read poetry and talked with a lilt. She had no family in the country and this was the only place for her to go. Bernie suffered from Alzheimer's, and somewhere in the conversation he became confused and thought we were talking about all going to live in Italy together. Every few minutes he interrupted to ask if he should go pack his suitcase.

The rugby was playing loudly on the television. Another man wore a bib and was being spoonfed by the nurse, who quietly cooed and chuckled with him.

I felt strange sitting here. Surely this was a scene from someone else's life, not mine?

Are we going to Italy? Let me get my suitcase. Are we going now? said Bernie.

I was surprised to see how my dad took the mealtime interactions in his stride. He talked to Bernie quietly, and considered what each person was saying, like he was back in his teaching days sitting with his students, even when Bernie spoke to him in gibberish. But also, sitting at this unfamiliar table in this strange new setting, I suddenly saw how small my father had become. The chemotherapy had made all his hair fall out, and his skull looked fragile, like an eggshell. The smaller he looked, the larger I felt. I was almost ashamed of my shining skin, my energy, all the space I was taking up.

Cut the umbilical cord, is what they say when a child is overly connected to their mother. But there is no piece of flesh that connects a father and daughter.

My dad got up from the dinner table and said, let's go out, and I started collecting everyone's plates. The nurse stopped me and said, it's raining outside, are you sure you want to go out there?

I looked to my dad, and he squeezed my arm and nodded. I told her I had brought an umbrella and that we would be fine. That felt strange too, that I had begun to do the communicating for us.

Suit yourselves, she said, but there's not much out there, and we stepped outside into the wet.

46

The beggars lie prostrated on each intersection on the grid of the central business district. They lie so their faces don't show, so they look like bundles of rags, the only indication they are human their arms, cupped and raised high to the sky to receive alms from a passerby.

Help, I've been mentally and physically abused the past ten years.

Help, I'm a recovering alcoholic and I have lost everything. Help me.

All these half-life stories squeezed onto a piece of cardboard. The lunchtime crowd steps over the beggars, ignoring them.

It doesn't suit our culture, Paul says to me, as we walk by on our way to a food court. It's too much. People don't respond well to seeing someone surrender and completely fall apart like that. We like to see a face. We want to engage. We like a fighter. We like a success story, like those other guys.

He points across the road to a man selling the *Big Issue*. The man banters with the suits and grins at the barrel-chested office men rushing past. Often, they stop, smile, offer him a broken-off piece of conversation, buy the magazine.

Paul points to another man who sits on a sleeping bag with his old kelpie. This man is known for reading science fiction, and sometimes people kneel down to talk to him about aliens, or how he thinks the world will end.

It's people like that, with their humour and humanity and

who can tell their story in a relatable way and make you feel part of their plight, says Paul. And there are amazing organisations who help give them their dignity back, you know. Not like the soggy bits of cardboard these other beggars have.

I murmur vaguely in agreement. But lately I have been wondering about the constant demand for stories, for complex lives to be packaged into neatly crafted and comprehensible narratives, ideally with a triumphant overcoming. Everything— advertisements, corporate biographies, mission statements, juice boxes—is personal narrative now, but flattened, far removed from the reality of living in the face of loss. And I wonder if there is a place in our world for the delicate, the quiet, the contradictory, the messy part of being.

When the inspirational story on the back of a cereal packet provokes tears, it's difficult not to harden yourself against the demand to feel all the time.

We sit in the food court and Paul tells me he won't be able to work with me again for a while. His baby is due next month. He will be taking on some full-time work as they need a more steady income and regular hours, and he needs to save.

It's the baby, he says, but it's not just that, you know. It turns out we want roots, we want a home, we want the small, everyday happiness. And we want to be able to give that feeling to our kid too. It seems like the biggest gift we could give them.

He asks me if I think I will continue with the freelance writing. I shrug and say I can't imagine what else I'd do at the moment. He says he is not sure if he will go back to it, with the baby and how frantic it will be and all, but also this lifestyle seems to breed its own form of loneliness.

I agree with him and say, sometimes my entire day can revolve around when to drink a coffee.

We look through the window at a man positioned under a sign that reads, Mick Simmons Sports Since 1977. He's sitting behind two milk crates stacked on top of each other, a dark blue cloth draped over the makeshift table. He wears a military jacket and sits still. People rush by and miss the writhing mass moving in front of him, the ball of fur, the glassy eye. On the table is a ferret.

But sometimes people stop. It is usually women. A young Japanese girl with a backpack and three-quarter pants and a broad gait that clashes with her delicate features stops and strokes the ferret. The man places the creature in her palms. He holds her hands, lingering slightly. She giggles silently as it moves. He pushes back her long hair and motions to her neck. She shakes her head, not understanding. He strokes her hair again and places the ferret in the crease between her neck and shoulder, and she shrieks, and he grabs the ferret, and she covers her mouth with her hand as though embarrassed that she made a sound of protest in the world.

Another time, two lesbians with tattoos run up and stroke the ferret and laugh and hold each other's hands, and ignore the man and walk off excited, while the man stares after them, nodding to himself.

But most of the time, people are looking anywhere but around them. We avert our eyes from strangers, outsiders, people who hang around aimlessly on street corners and park benches. The lost of the city. The flotsam waiting for the tides to change the direction of their lives. The ones we do not speak of when we build our expanding myth of a sparkling city.

47

Andy's girlfriend has ended things with him. But he says it is good. He says he is cleansing himself, finally getting old patterns out of his system. He says the parties and the drugs and the midnight rides were decomposing his soul.

We are sitting on the floor of his room, barefoot and cross-legged. He has been getting into therapeutic massage, and has been reading about reiki and minimalism, so now there's no furniture. He has just returned from Thailand, and he is saying it was easier there. I can't put my finger on it, he says, but every time I come back, after a holiday or living abroad, I think, why is it so hard here?

I ask him if the difference is that he's always on holidays when he's away, whereas here he works. He gives me a look and says, sure, there might be that, but I just feel a darkness here when I first come back. And then it goes away. Or I acclimatise. I love this place, because of memories and because of what I've made here. But when I break my patterns, I also see I have a dysfunctional relationship with this city, and it's one that's so easy to fall back into.

There are places in the world, he says, where the frequencies of energies all rumble and whoosh into one place. Sacred places, where magic can happen. Dark places where other kinds of magic can occur too. He says he has been reading that every city has a frequency, a different way of resonating.

He tells me he has been thinking about places on the planet

where the magnetic lines cross and gather energy and create high vibration points, like Stonehenge or Incan monuments or the island of Es Vedrà, and about lost places like the drowned city of Atlantis.

Andy says he wants to find out what the vibrational frequency of Sydney is, to understand why he feels this way.

Thing is, this is a beautiful city, he says. But a lot of people say there is something off here and that it is difficult to connect with others.

It is true. People smile a lot here. But it is not a city where you can easily make a friend. We are friendly. Not curious. We will ask how you are, but turn before you have finished explaining. Travellers say how beautiful it is. And how hard it can be to become close to people.

People talk about soul cities, or cities that speak to them. Sydney, despite its beauty, has never made me feel settled in my bones. Sure, its landscape informs my being, but it is not a city in tune with my internal rhythms. This is an outdoor city, but we keep our desires, our doubts, our hearts hidden behind locked screen doors. We have parks, we have space, we gorge on natural beauty. Weekend coastal walks, beers by the beach, dog walks in the sun. People walk up and down the sandy coastline, but it is so difficult to read the emotional state of the city; people keep their feelings politely locked up.

We joke a lot as though we know we're on borrowed time, on borrowed land. But I wonder, how can we learn to grieve for ourselves if our country doesn't know how to grieve its own history?

Once in a while, Andy and I both agree, when there is a bushfire, and the nation is gripped by panic, the snap-crackle-and-pop heat forces the flowers to erupt out of their hiding, and there, exposed and blazing for a moment, is the fire and destruction that lies tightly bound up in our easygoing hearts.

There is a huge crack outside. We open the front door and

watch as the rain comes thundering down, tropical, furious, drenching the inner-city streets, and two girls and a man walking his dog all break into a run, while the moon throws a watery glow over them.

It's like it knows we are speaking about it, Andy whispers. And we both go silent, like chastised kids, and watch as people rush under shop awnings and hide from the power of this land.

48

There came a time in the final months when my dad decided to give away some of his books.

He had invited three of his friends around and asked me to join them. My mother and his friends and I sat in the spring sunshine in the backyard while flowers dropped around us and we drank coffee.

Suddenly out of nowhere for us, though he had clearly thought about it, my dad came out with some of his most special books to give to his friends. The act in itself was nothing that strange. But these were books he held dearly. He had chosen a soul-book for each of his friends: *Capital* by Thomas Piketty, *Memoirs of a Revolutionary* by Victor Serge, *Prima che il gallo canti* by Cesar Pavese.

And even though something dark and lumpy caught in my throat, I felt I needed to support his wants and my mother, so I asked each friend to pose with the book that defined their relationship with my father, and I took a snap, like a mugshot.

But something shifted when my father asked them if they wanted more books, and he began bringing out his collector's editions of Dante and sets of Italian verses in thick leather binding. He started pulling books off his shelf, frantically, as though he were shedding his skin.

And I saw the way one of those friends looked at the collectable books, a look of love that seemed to value the books above my father, and for that betrayal, for the briefest of moments, I hated him.

Another friend, a woman, who might have read something from my body language or in my mother's silence, looked distressed, and she said, this is not right, you can't give these away, this is not goodbye, this is too soon. And she kept repeating it.

It is too soon, it is too soon, it is too soon.

And for that, for the briefest of moments, I loved her.

49

Someone we know is having a party at a small bar, and Katie convinces me to go.

You have been so hard to reach, she says.

I walk into the bar, which is covered in plants and giant fronds, and find that all my friends have been transformed into magical nymphs by make-up and the drinks and the power of the night.

Faces assemble before me from different stages in my life, but there is no one I feel particularly drawn towards. Features blur, and I am filled with a sense of dread at the questions I will have to answer through the night, and I feel resentful about things no one has even asked me yet.

My housemates are here somewhere, along with friends from high school, and people I know by sight but have never really spoken to. By this point, in this pocket of Sydney, it feels like all my worlds have merged and all the friends are friends of friends. We have shared histories that go nowhere. I guess this is what happens when you stay in one place long enough.

A guy that I knew back at school comes up to us. His hair-line is receding and his face looks emaciated. I remember hearing from somewhere that he deals drugs now and is always having affairs with younger and younger girls.

Wow, Katie whispers, he looks terrible.

He sidles up to us, inhaling intensely from his vape pen. He doesn't say anything, just blows a thin line of vape smoke in our direction.

Eventually he turns to speak to me. My mum sent me something you wrote in the paper.

There is a beat. Katie and I wait for him to take a drag on his pen.

I haven't read it though, he says, shrugging. He exhales.

Dickhead, mutters Katie under her breath.

We see a girl we know standing by an outdoor heater. She waves at us and as we go over to her I say to Katie, he seems pretty down on life. She rolls her eyes and says, don't let him start making you feel bad for him. You always do this. You like to find the people that everyone writes off and convince yourself of their unknown suffering, and that it makes them somehow interesting.

That's not true, I say. And she laughs and says, it's like your party trick.

My phone beeps. It's a message from Paul—It's a girl!—with a photo of his girlfriend holding a tiny swaddled baby. Under the picture is an emoji of a smiley face with heart eyes. I am happy for him, but I also feel so distant from this idea of joy and a new life. Mechanically I message back an exploding heart.

We walk up to the girl we know and she waggles a glinting finger at us. We both squeal and hug her. She looks at us and says, I'm finally doing it, and she gives a strange giggle. We raise our glasses, to her and to the new apartment they are buying with their combined income and a loan from both sets of parents to mark the occasion.

We exchange words like equity and bonds, and talk about how hard it is for people in our generation to break into the property market, while I think about the word mortgage, and how its meaning is death pledge. Another girl in the group says, I have news also, and shares that she has been tipped to receive a promotion later in the year.

I raise my glass to these girlfriends who are growing up

before my eyes and plotting their own idea of a buffer against those wild and uncertain lands of the future.

I wander inside to the small dance floor, where a few people I recognise are shuffling their hips, swaying, and a couple are grinding against each other. A pretty boy is on stage, playing electronic tunes from his MacBook.

While the others are dancing, I stand, holding up the wall. I am sure I used to have a good time at parties, but I think even back in the day these kinds of gatherings exhausted me, and I always felt like everyone knew some secret to having fun that I didn't.

I remember years ago when I visited Rome, to see the city my father lived in during his bachelor years, and I saw Bernini's Apollo and Daphne. One by one her limbs had solidified into the hard, barky roots of a laurel tree so she could escape Apollo. But the thing that most struck me was her face, frozen in marbled terror, her moment of shock and even fear at her fate. She preferred to sacrifice herself; anything was better than losing her sense of will or control. I have been feeling my own sense of control slipping away from me this past year. I wonder whether my limbs are turning into a tree, or if I am closer to hardening into marble.

I'm feeling faint and I realise I should eat something, and it will give me something to do. I order the only vegetarian thing on the pub menu, an expensive salad. When it comes it is just a few pieces of cos lettuce, some slices of pear, and a drizzle of ponzu.

I sit down alone on the corner of a bench and poke the lettuce with my fork. Next to me, I hear a hacking laugh accompanied by the mist of a vape.

That's a pretty shit salad, I hear.

I'm really not in the mood, I say, not looking up.

Look, if it makes you feel any better, I ordered a triple bacon and cheese burger, so I'll probably get clogged arteries and die.

Why, I ask, stabbing a pear, would that make me feel better?

'Cause I'll suffer. He coughs for a while, and then sits down next to me saying, that seems enough to make most people happy.

I don't think your suffering would make anyone happy, I say. Plus, your clogged arteries make no difference to my salad experience. There is no relationship between the two.

He throws me a long look.

I think you're wrong about that. Lots of people take great pleasure in other's misfortunes. It boosts their sense of self and ego and the idea that they're doing something right. That's a pretty clear relationship. I know people like to hear it when I screw up, anyway. That's why I never set up anyone's expectations. Especially women. They always get disappointed.

Well, maybe you should stop fucking underage girls then, I say.

He snorts. You're not so bad, you know. And we are silent for a while as I eat my salad.

I heard your old man passed away, he says after a while.

I feel a thudding in my chest, and I give a weird shrug with my shoulders to stop myself saying anything as I don't trust my voice with my feelings.

I wind my legs tightly around the bench, like evergreen tree creepers, hoping for the night to envelop me and decide my fate in its magic. I sit like this for a while.

Finally, without looking at him, I say, why, does my hurt make you feel better?

He eventually shrugs his shoulders and inhales from his vape. Not really, no. I'm sorry. And we look up at each other for a moment, and then he exhales and starts to cough.

50

On a Sunday, all my housemates are out and I can feel something threatening under my skin. I've learned it's important in these moments to keep moving or the feeling will overtake me. I grab a backpack and shove in a water bottle, phone charger, and jumper, and take the next train out west towards the bush and the mountains.

An hour and a half later, I get off at Katoomba station, and use Google Maps to guide me to the start of a famous Blue Mountain walk. All around me are signals we are moving out of winter: wildflowers are blooming and small fairy-wrens hop between trees. In the city, the seasons blur into each other, but out here I can feel a distinct shift.

When I arrive at the visitors centre, there are loads of buses and tourists piled up in the carpark heading towards the look-out point. I think about how people make pilgrimages and line up to look into canyons, blowholes, fjords, and valleys. It speaks to something eternal in all of us and I wonder what they are searching for.

I shuffle away from the throngs of people and walk the opposite way down a trail with steep ledges. I walk for about two hours with my head bowed down.

My mum called this week and suggested I come to India. She said I should take some time off from running around, paying bills, and striving so hard to be someone. She said sometimes it is okay to be looked after.

It's tempting. I am not quite sure what is keeping me here

at the moment. But something is still tugging at me. I switched to speaker and let the silence grow as I stared at the mug on my bedside table with its small patterns of blue fish swimming around the rim.

When I look up, I am at the edge of a quiet mountain look-out with signs telling me to tread carefully and to mind the dangerous steep cliff.

The sun is going down, and everywhere is light, and I try to shade my eyes. I cannot handle it, this light, there is so much of it.

And I remember how, towards the end, I was talking with my dad and his friend, an older lapsed Catholic, in my parents' backyard. They were talking about people who were going to Syria to fight against Assad, and whether the government was right or not to stop people from going.

I don't give a shit what side people want to be on, his friend was saying. I can't support anything done in the name of advancing religion. I've seen enough. The West's foreign policy has been the best thing for Islam. It's made the religion alive and relevant again. Look at what's happening in Turkey and how everything is changing there. I hate that.

We have only ever supported foreign conflict before, my dad said. Even when we boarded everything up, we have never felt the true stress or apprehension of the blown-up train tunnel, of the Harbour Bridge crumbling, of bombs dropping on our heads.

It has never been that clear to me, my dad went on, who the real enemy is in any war. During the Second World War people at least felt they were defending their own country, standing up for Australia, which I can understand. But this is so different. Young people from our own country want to join foreign wars to fight against the West. At some point, we have to turn inwards and look at ourselves, and our own country, and ask how we got to this point. How is it we have young people here who want to fight against us? And that's something no one wants to think about.

We are all standing in the shadow of a great fear, his friend said. This is a new era, his friend said, and they both looked at me.

As the night went on, they both talked about getting older, and what kept them going, and the wars they had lived through. And his friend was saying it was things like politics and people and his children and his magnolia tree that kept him going. But eventually he said that, deep down in his heart, his biggest fear was that on his deathbed he might turn back to Him again.

I asked my father what he believed in, and if he wanted to go to church now.

I'm too far gone for that, he said. I can't return to it just because I need it. But I believe in words, he said. And I believe in music. And I take great, great comfort from this.

But that's stupid, I wanted to say. Words are so fickle. You can't put your faith in something that shifts and morphs and that can't be pinned down.

The thing is, my father said, we take solace in whatever small thing we can, because at our core, we are all scared of losing the things we have. He reached across and squeezed my hand.

And I listened that night as they continued to speak about religion and faith as though it were linear, as though it were something they could choose to go back to, or to move towards.

Many of my friends and I were taught to question all belief systems, but taught little about how to believe, and lately I've found myself thinking that surely something grander must be offered to us, but I don't know in what direction I can move to try to find it.

I look down into the pit of sandstone as bars of light stretch across the silvery winter gums and it makes me tremble. Staring into a valley is like a glimpse into the exposed gut of the earth.

Shouldn't you be stronger than this? I scream at the cracking earth. I hear my voice bounce along the walls of the surrounding mountains.

I realise my face is wet with tears, and I look away from the valley as sometimes it is unbearable, unspeakable, to witness such vulnerability in your land.

I wipe my face and grab my backpack, and despite the fact that the sun still bathes me I know the world will always be a little less bright now, and I scramble behind the rocks and let the darkened silhouettes shade me.

51.

L ately I've found that the house has been big enough for
me to hide in and I haven't really been interacting with
my housemates.

The last few months, I have felt a growing shame that they
have been witnessing me dissolve, and it has made me avoid
them. I just want to lie in bed and listen to the rain tumble on
the roof and the wind sigh between the bare branches. I often
feel that wave of grief that is something like exhaustion and
apathy mixed together. I imagine it milky to the touch. I can't
predict when it will appear, and so I have been cancelling my
plans, but I don't know what excuse to give, so I normally
mumble something like, oh, I can't make it anymore, which
then makes the friend I was meeting frustrated. It seems easier
just not to make the plan at all. And I feel almost a relief that I
can give my days over to memories of old friends and times and
live instead in the past.

I'm not sure if they have noticed, as everyone is busy. We
don't need to tell each other where we are going, with who, or
when we will be back; we can come and go with the kind of
freedom that I had always dreamed of when I was younger. We
can go days, even weeks, without properly seeing each other.
Sometimes this feels strange, and I am not sure if everyone is
still connected or if there have been small hurts that were never
resolved. Apart from the basics, like keeping stuff clean, we
have no real obligations to one another.

Our house WhatsApp group used to be filled with in-jokes

and small comments about our days. But lately it has been used mainly for logistics: the electricity bill has come in; can everyone please pay me back for the condiments; the cleaner will arrive next Thursday morning.

The only times we've seen each other recently have been unplanned and unexpected. Like I might be coming back from work with no plans and not sure what to do with the looming evening ahead, and I will open the door, and Niki will be there cooking a pot of pasta and talking on the phone all laughing and flushed, and will pause and call out, hey do you want any? And suddenly the flutter of panic I had about my unfolding evening filled with memories and the milky feelings will dissolve, and be replaced with the comfort of a home-cooked meal. We will sit at our long wooden kitchen table, which we picked up on a council clean-up day, and Niki will put out two ceramic bowls for pasta and a wooden bowl for salad, and outside it will be growing darker as she tells me about her latest date or her scheme for a new career path.

I don't know if this is how other people feel when they come home after losing something important in their lives—the fear of the dark, stretched-out evenings and the relief of an interaction about where to buy discount designer swimmers—but when moments like these happen, I feel a warmth through me, like I am a part of something.

I try to rest nonchalantly against the counter, or run my hands through my hair, so I also appear casual, like this is normal for me too. So she won't notice the extent of my gratitude for these small human connections.

We can be so busy chasing the extraordinary that we forget the ache of the small; little things like the phone messages I would receive from my father, who was so fazed by technology that he would somehow always hang up in the middle of a sentence, and I would roll my eyes when I listened to it, or the midweek emails he would send me asking for a dinner date, or the way his fingers were always cool. I miss the ordinariness of feeling part of a family.

And while Niki talks about her passive-aggressive boss, and updates me on her sister who she was just talking with on the phone, she will reach across and squeeze my hands and give a small smile, and I will eat the hot buttery pasta and nod and let her talk, because listening to a person who is a part of the day-to-day world can be one of the most comforting things.

52.

O ne month before my father passed, he asked me to come visit him in the hospital alone.

There had been construction work outside the hospital for some weeks. I felt the drilling outside reverberate and loosen and tug at the city's core as I walked through the ward.

It was late afternoon and he was wrapped under the hospital sheets. He shuffled himself up on a pillow when he saw me.

Is it a sea-creature day? I asked. He smiled back faintly and said, today feels more like a bottom-feeder kind of day.

In my bag my phone pinged with messages and emails and as I reached for it he asked me what my plans were for the future. I didn't know what to say. I knew that what he was really asking was if I was going to be okay without him. And I didn't know how to answer that truthfully.

The rest of the world had already started to swirl around me by this stage; I had begun to feel out of sync with my twenty-something peers and more in tune with the elderly, the schoolchildren, the unemployed, the sick, anyone who dared to walk at an abnormal pace.

I squeezed onto the bed and lay next to him, both of us leaning against the pillow.

He had a stack of books on his bedside table. There were books on mythology, politics, world history, short stories. I laughed and said, you clearly still have ambition, and he smiled. I picked one up. He said he just liked to know they were there, next to him, like friends. He told me that all the medication meant he couldn't concentrate on the words and now they just blurred on the page.

He said he couldn't hold a pen anymore, so there was nowhere to put his thoughts; the dark shapes were roaming loose and unguarded around his head.

What is the point of living, then, he said, smiling softly and gesturing vaguely at his hospital gown, the monitor, the catheter, his bald head.

I opened one of his books, a collection of short stories by Henry James, and I turned to his favourite ghost story and began reading aloud, like he had done for me thousands of times before.

Overhead the fan whirred gently as he drifted in and out of sleep. I wriggled further down the bed and suddenly I was six years old again, taking midweek afternoon naps with my dad. The fan rustled the sheet while time tugged at us and folded into itself.

I didn't know where else I wanted to be, except there with him. His hand came out from under the sheet and patted along the side of the bed, searching for mine. I held it. It was cool and soft, and his skin was paper-thin. I could feel his mind going to another invisible place where I could not follow. I looked out the window. In the distance the harbour bent and wrapped itself closer to the land. The city was shifting before my eyes.

Blood and mortar; bone and water. Why are you leaving and making me stay?

I listened to him sleeping next to me, as fine silt and shale drifted in the wind, and quarries filled, and the sun left the sky, and the street lamps switched on.

53

The day after my dad died, I went to the ocean pool at Bronte. Sydney is littered with ocean pools; they sit safely nestled away from the hazardous waves. The day was heavy and humid and it stuck to my skin as I waited for the summer storm to hit. The clouds thickened and darkened. The air swelled. The ocean churned.

I dived into the water. Sea urchins and anemones and small fish danced below me.

When I was a kid, I once had a bad fever for a week and my mind went into hallucinations. I remember being convinced my dad had died. I walked into the television room where he was watching the news. And I went up to him, and asked him why he had left me. He held me and said he was still here, but in my mind I knew he was lying and I kept repeating that he was a ghost, and that this is what ghosts do, try to convince you that they are still here.

It took him a long time to calm me down, and then he put me back into bed, and his hands, which were always soft and cool, stroked my brow for what felt like hours.

I swam laps up and down, up and down, until the bruised sky above me broke. The rain met the ocean, and it was hard to tell which way was up, and which way was down, because everywhere was water and water and water, and it felt like there would never be land again.

SPRING

54

I am waiting in line at a discount chemist in Broadway. It is midweek and it has been hot for days and people's nerves are running high so they are crowding into the air-conditioned malls. It is school holidays and teenagers are everywhere. It makes everything louder, but it is nice to be injected with all this wired energy, the swagger and swearing and slang that is normally shut away during the week, so that without it sometimes the city feels like it's just old people and babies and one beat. I watch a trio of boys jostle each other as they ride up the escalator following a young woman in a short skirt and I feel their thrill of desire.

In front of me a woman in her sixties is making some small fuss and holding up the queue. She has bought an array of items and there seems to be some confusion about how to transport them. The cashier has an accent, maybe Spanish, and seems confused. She is asking the woman if she wants a bag, a plastic bag, to put her things into.

No, no, no, the woman is saying. I don't approve of plastic.

Okay, says the cashier, but the older woman looks frazzled and confused, and says she has no bag of her own. Again she is offered a plastic bag, and again she snaps, no, and the cashier looks concerned and says, but then where will you put them, and holds out some of the items.

The woman lunges suddenly and grabs the items from the cashier brusquely, and there is a clunk as some of the cosmetics drop on the floor, and the woman looks startled and looks at the cashier and almost yells at her, just hand me that plastic bag, she says, and shoves all her items in it and huffs away.

I am next in line and the cashier woman looks like she is about to cry.

You heard me, she says to me, you heard me, right, I asked her if she wanted a bag so many times? I definitely said this, no?

I say, yes, you did, it's okay, I heard you. But she still looks so distressed.

People here, they are always yelling or upset by something, she says. Today this woman, and before that a man who wanted these wax earplugs and he couldn't find the brand or something that he liked so he just starts yelling out of nowhere. What is all this anger about? I don't understand, can people not understand my accent?

I tell her that her accent is not a problem.

I need my visa, she continues, and so I need to stay working here but I don't understand why people are upset and always in this hurry. I thought this was relaxed place. Now I am upset too.

I want to say something to soothe this woman trapped in her modern-day apothecary, but I am not sure what that might be, so I just look at her, and repeat that it is okay, and I tell her not to worry so much. People are weird, I say.

And she stares at me.

People. Are. Weird. She repeats this back to me slowly.

She takes the face cream I've been holding out to scan it. As she is scanning she says it again, and she starts smiling. And then suddenly she is laughing. She is laughing and saying, yes, this, it is so true, this is exactly it, people are weird.

She offers me the machine for my card, and she is still laughing, and she smiles at me, and I smile back at her, and it's as if some valve has broken, and suddenly we both cannot stop laughing, and she doesn't offer me a bag, and instead she just keeps laughing, both of us repeating, people are weird, and we laugh into the air-conditioned chemist, as the boys travel back down the escalator, high-fiving each other and whooping with joy.

55

S ami has been offered a job in Dubai. He asks me for coffee, and at a local cafe he tells me that it starts next year and he thinks he will take it. It is strange, he says, my parents actually want me to take it.

I figure they think I'm more likely to meet someone I can marry there, he says, and maybe I agree with them.

It is still a job in law, but, he says, it's important to change just one thing at a time. Too many changes and you feel scared, or don't know what to appreciate, he says.

My eyes start to well up and he gives my hand a squeeze. I know that of course I cannot hold him back just because I find goodbyes so hard. And I also feel happy that he has decided to follow one of his dreams, even if it means things will change again.

He tells me he is excited to go to the Middle East and to read more poetry. He likes to write poems too, he says, and it surprises me that I didn't know this about him before.

I know mine aren't any good, he says, and I don't have ambitions for them, but I like to write them, and I would like to learn how to write them better.

He says he never wanted to admit to guys at school or university that he read poetry.

It has a different tradition here, he says. People seem to think only queer guys or actors read it, or something. But Rumi, Iqbal, Hafiz, we grew up with these men quoted to us like gods.

I would like to be able to write about things that I don't know how to explain, he says. All the things that sometimes make me feel forced into a position before I even know how I feel about it. Like with my parents. Or with women. Or Islam. Or even half the legal cases I work on, which are just about being able to make words fit an argument. Or is it the other way around, I never know.

I would love to be able to write a poem that doesn't fit into anything, he continues. Maybe about what it felt like when I went to Palestine for the first time with my sister. And how the white-and-blue Israeli checkpoint flags somehow look different in person than they do on television. Or how we crossed the border from Jordan in the back of an old green Soviet car that had squeaky brakes, or how some of the soldiers at the checkpoint were the same age as I was, and how I looked into the eyes of one young boy, who looked so anxious even as he clenched his loaded AK47, or how there were so many people waiting at the checkpoint and anxiety was bouncing off the walls, or how in the middle of this I suddenly had a craving for the local bitter olives. Or how there was this feeling in the air, like. Something. Is. Going. To. Happen. I was told later by my cousin who lives in Jordan that that is often what it feels like to return home.

I would like to be able to write about nothing and everything really, Sami says. And maybe I will.

I say that maybe this move will be a good thing, to change the way his mind has become wired here.

And he nods and says, yes, maybe in Dubai I will write something that is for no one and for everyone.

56

Tessa is visiting from Los Angeles, where she has been living the past few years, trying to make it as an actress. We are at the Dawn Fraser Baths in Balmain. We used to swim at these baths before we could drive, when the ocean felt too far away to get to by the long trail of buses. From the harbour you can hear the creak of the tethered boats. The harbour water sounds different from the open ocean; there's a slight industrial rumble here, a sort of weariness through the water.

Tessa is confused about whether to stay or go back.

I mean, this is where I want to raise my family, she says. I want my kids to spend weekends barefoot on the sand, and to actually have access to healthcare and education. But I'm also excited. About the new opportunities over there and about having new conversations, you know.

We tread water and I nod my head.

I last came here over a year ago, after my dad was moved to the palliative care ward, the week before he died.

The palliative section was much more peaceful that the rest of the hospital. The urgent bustle and beeps and bings of machinery were replaced by the sounds of soft breathing, quiet calm. No one rushed. There was no need. The windows were large and expansive, there was a courtyard, and pot plants were everywhere, tendrils of plant matter defiantly living on. Tea was plentiful. You didn't have to stress about hospital parking, as all-day permits were handed out to family.

In the kitchen, families spoke together quietly, with respect and care, people who understood and asked each other about their loved ones. This was the place that existed between worlds. Here was the world of goodbyes—to each other, to the world of the living, to the land of suffering.

Tessa and I get out of the water and lie down on the wooden slats, closing our eyes, our bodies drenched in sunlight. We listen as two girls in the water near us shout as the tide brings in fleshy, transparent blobs of jellyfish. I hear one of the girls squeal, I touched one, I touched one.

Tessa laughs and says, they remind me of us when we were younger. Remember when we would come down here at night and skinny-dip under the Moreton Bay figs and totally freak out when the jellyfish brushed up against us?

What would you do on a perfect day, we hear one of the girls ask the other, and there's a splash of water, and the friend replies, this.

Yeah, but what if money wasn't an issue, insists the girl, and you could go anywhere you wanted?

There is a pause.

Mmm, still this, the friend says dreamily. This is all I want, to live like this.

Tessa reaches her hand out to mine as we listen to the creak of the jetty and the girlish chatter, and the harbour water gently moans its stories beneath us.

57

More than two years ago, before my father became ill, I visited some friends in London.

It takes twenty-two hours to fly to London with a layover stop. You are so far away, people say somewhat accusingly, as if amazed that in this modern world that blips and fizzes by under our control, we still can't move the tectonic plates any closer. Our geography seems to deny technological progress as we keep drifting further and further apart.

My London friends all moved at a frenzied pace, screeching along the tube, jumping out at Earl's Court and laughing, and hurtling onto the tube waiting across the platform, quickly, before the doors shuts.

It all felt like this, quickly, quickly, before the door shuts, squeezing, slotting, shooting in with glee, no waiting at lights, nimbly dancing between the moving traffic, always somewhere to be, scarves trailing behind us in the autumn briskness.

And hello, there you are, and what excitement as we crashed into the warm bookstores, and pubs, and late-night gigs, bumping into friends because we were all birds of a feather in the night.

Colours drain away in that city of watered-down grey silhouettes. There is nothing to capture the eye, until night, when the lights come on.

One night, I was talking to a French-Canadian dancer who was a lodger with a local family, and I remember thinking, what an old word. She said she felt she was piggybacking on their lives, to the point where she has started to dislike them.

It's not healthy for your sense of self, she said, to be cast as the lodger, an outsider, the watcher who pays to sit alongside the lives others build.

She told me the husband in the family was Australian, and we were discussing how the Australian psyche is so opposed to reflection, and how she struggled with his tunnel-vision politics, and I said feebly, oh, but not all Australians are like this.

Of course, she said, but there is an outwardness to all the Australians I've met, a lack of interiority, maybe because you live on coastal edges, which is sort of exhausting isn't it?

I agreed and then felt guilty, like I should have stood up for my country and my people more, but I have never known how to defend something when I am so criss-crossed in my mind.

I said, there is so much about the country that is beautiful.

Of course, she said, waving her hand dismissively, you have to love it, or it would be rather self-loathing of you, wouldn't it?

Is that true: is a feeling about a city also a feeling about oneself? And if so, how does one ever separate their city from themselves? Are we all superimposing ourselves onto our backdrop, forcing the geography to come alive with our own loss and love?

I looked at the little dancer, who was maybe in her mid-thirties, and I wondered how long her body would let her keep dancing professionally.

She said she might head home because she, and we, were all tired from the night, and I suddenly and unexpectedly longed for my city under that great unhealthy hole in the sky, where the sun tattoos you.

58

L ast night Bowerbird had his EP launch. Niki went, but both Sami and I had to work, so he is telling us about it over lunch. I ask if he felt the ocean, and his eyes brighten and he says, oh yes.

He says it was very humbling to have his friends and loved ones with him. My sister couldn't come, he says, and looks a bit sad.

But, he tells us, there has been good news and the doctors think they can make her better. I give him a hug.

He says the doctors are always quick to say that nothing can be certain, that they cannot make any promises. Really, no one can make promises about anything in life, he says, and the poor doctors bear this inhuman weight. But it is disconcerting nonetheless, as if your lover said to you daily that they were not certain for how long they could promise their love to you. It is all true, he says, but it doesn't mean that's what I always want to be told or how I want to live.

Sami asks about the next step. Do you record an album now?

And Bowerbird shrugs and says, I guess so.

It's strange, he says, I thought this night would be the climax to some stage in my life. Or some kind of definitive punctuation mark. At least a colon. So much has changed this year, but also nothing has really changed. And I can't tell if I feel incredible disappointment or relief. The days are exactly the same, except now I just have to create a new goal to work towards, like an album, which I will probably do. And then I will pursue that for the next one or two years, and I will probably achieve that too. And on that day in two years I will be sitting with you both, or maybe with two different people entirely in a different share house, and it will feel like this again. That's what all this next, next, next, boils down to, really. Is that sad? Or is it the most freeing thing, that none of it really matters that much?

Sami says he thinks this is why it is important to celebrate small wins along the way. He says if we don't take the time to do that for every small act we have managed, no matter how small or insignificant it might seem to the outside world, well, only then is it sad.

We decide to go to the bar down the road, the one the filmmaker's son owns, and we buy a beer from him, and sit on a crate outside, and cheers to Bowerbird and to the small things.

59

Andy has started online dating. He says he is finally joining the masses. He says in the five years he was with his girlfriend all the rules have changed. I feel old, he says. But also, it's amazing to have access to a whole network of people that I would never otherwise get to meet.

He has come over and we are sitting at the kitchen table drinking mugs of tea, with a strange assortment of savoury biscuits and nuts and some spreads and a tube of mayonnaise from my cupboard in front of us. I was raised to always offer food when guests come over—even if it's unannounced, like Andy's visit was. But the share-house fridge is usually in a state of bareness or disgrace, so while I try to stay true to my roots, it often means there are some strange offerings and I don't think my ancestors would approve.

He says the thing he doesn't like about dating is the games. And he senses the girl he is seeing now is playing some kind of power game with him.

The first time we met for a drink, there were sparks, he tells me. And the second time we met she kissed me. And last night, we went out for dinner at Jazzsushi, which was expensive, and I don't mind paying, except for the fact that she acted bored and aloof the whole time.

Niki comes home and she sits down with us and starts spreading a water cracker with peanut butter.

Did she kiss you? she asks

Yeah. I mean, we slept together.

Well, there's your answer, right?

But it was strange, he says. I couldn't tell if she was wait-ing for me to do something more, or if it was some kind of control thing, or if she didn't want to sleep with me at all, so afterwards I sort of left. I don't think I'll message her again.

What, says Niki, like, no message at all? You won't text something?

Well, she didn't seem keen. She kept staring off into the dis-tance and she'd give me these tight smiles. And she ate a lot of sushi, she even ordered the special roll with salt and pepper crab, so I kind of feel like my role is done. I think I'll leave it, otherwise it's just awkward.

You can't just ghost her, says Niki. It pisses me off when guys do that, like, you spent all this time together and you slept with her and then nothing. Not even a message because you feel awkward. Fuck, I feel so dispensable.

It's probably a much riskier experience for women, he says, and I can only imagine the kind of shit you get, but in my expe-rience the no texting back thing after sleeping together hap-pens from both genders, big time. I've had it done to me, it cuts both ways.

To be fair, I say to Niki, you did the same thing with that last guy.

Yeah, okay, but he was saying weird things about how much he liked my skin and kept asking what products I used. I got underlying Asian fetish, or killer—at best narcissist—vibes from him.

We have all said something promising on a date and then not responded to texts because we don't want to let someone down, I say.

I mean, dating can be a pretty hollowing experience, Andy says. When I was in the Uber coming home afterwards, I just felt so flat. Like, way lower than I should about some girl who

I had just met. I'm not even sure if I was sad about her exactly. Maybe I'm just not ready to date.

We pick at the biscuits at the table and are silent for a while.

I think it's the hope, I say, finally. It takes so much courage, I think, to get up, meet with another human, show up, and then share parts of our lives with each other. In a few dates, you find out about their jobs, and their days, their siblings and families and memories from their childhood. We judge and blame and notice all their weird tics, and try to get as much information out of them as we can to assess if we want to take it any further. And then don't text. And that's a special kind of rejection. It's so intimate and it takes so much courage for both people. And it's something about the hope we are all trading on. And we don't talk much about that part.

Niki gives me a little hug. It's true, she says. I get super down on myself because I don't want to be seen wanting. And I want to put that armour on. But still, we do jump back in because there's hope. And that is probably one of the most beautiful things about us.

Yeah, Andy is saying, maybe I will text her to say I'm not interested. I mean, I feel a bit shit admitting this, but I will probably start swiping other women again tonight. I am not sure if that is beautiful, but I do like thinking about it as hope and that we are both feeling that way. It's a kinder way to be towards people who cross our lives, I guess.

My phone rings and I see it is my mum, so I excuse myself to answer. She asks how I am and updates me on the aunties and family and tells me about a trip to a temple she visited once with my father.

Remember that place we had the fish with the banana leaves? she asks. It had that tamarind sauce, but it was so simple.

Yes, I say. We ate it with our hands, sitting at a plastic table and chair.

A few years ago, we had been in India staying with family for some months and one day my mum and I decided to go further south for a few days. And that day, while eating this fish and drinking lemon soda, we had both collapsed into silly giggles, the type that come on when you have been away from the familiar for too long and the whole world suddenly feels bizarre.

I think I'm ready to come back to Sydney now, she says. I miss home.

I am silent, but I feel some air returning to my lungs. And as that little bubble rises, I realise how much I have squashed down any of my own feelings of hope in the past two years.

That was a good day, I say finally. And my mum is silent on the other end, but I can feel that she, too, is smiling and replaying that day in her mind.

60

It is a Sunday and the heat is draining and we have all had a bad week.

Sami will be leaving for Dubai very soon, at the end of the year, but there has been a small visa complication and he is feeling anxious. Bowerbird has decided to move in with cafe girl, but he is questioning whether it is too soon and so they just had a fight about it.

I tell her it has only been a year, he says, but she keeps saying, exactly, almost a whole year, and I think maybe we have different ideas of what a year signifies.

Niki and I were thinking about keeping the house, but once the landlord found out a new lease needed to be signed they put the price up and now neither of us can afford it. We are going to try to find another place together, but both of us have agreed that if some good offer comes up for either of us, we should take it. Housing is hard, she says, shrugging, we've got to take what we can sometimes.

Each of us has become caught up in our own thoughts and worries and in planning the next steps towards the unknown future.

We are lying sprawled on bean bags or against the cool floor tiles, and Sami has the brilliant idea to bring in a fan, and we let out a small cheer as he sets up the breeze against our bodies.

We start listing all the ocean pools we can think of, half in an attempt to muster the energy to go to one, and half hoping that just by naming them it will cool us down. Shelly Beach. McIver's. Northbridge Baths.

On Thursday nights, we have started going to a dance night at an old church where all the windows have been covered up with cardboard and gaffer tape, and there are no lights. Inside a DJ plays loud dance music, but it's not obscure electro or house stuff, it's classic stuff, like the pop stuff you know would get you kicked out of a warehouse party if you admitted to liking it. But your body doesn't know the difference, it just feels the beat and the soundtrack of its younger days and starts moving.

People fumble to find a little patch of space that is theirs. And then we just dance. All limbs and knees, and salsa, and body rolls, and stuff we never learned professionally, but again, the body doesn't know this, and it believes it can move with the best of them, and cuts big shapes, so that for a moment in time we can forget about what limits us outside in the light.

Newport, says Sami.

Um. The old man ones out at Maroubra, says Niki. And the ones where women get naked at Coogee.

Yeah, that's McIver's, it's already been said, says Bowerbird.

On some days, we sit around sipping tea and mocking people who cling to their objects. We congratulate ourselves on our castaway pots and pans, and used mattresses, and antique mirror frames, and revolving share-house doors, and hand-me-down backpacks, and overflowing dress-up boxes for parties. On those days we Google council clean-up days in the rich suburbs of Sydney and all cram into a GoGet ute to pick at other people's discarded trash, like gleeful young vultures.

Avalon. Curl Curl. Cremorne Point. Mc-something. Malabar.

On other evenings, Niki and Sami and Bowerbird and I find ourselves watching slick furniture ads. I marvel at the woman our age, confidently splayed over her new creamy beige lounge. So sure of herself, because she has a couch, in a home, and there is a white curly dog in the corner, and a man walks past in the background, and she gives a knowing smile, as if by the very act of couch ownership she has cheated death itself. Her existence feels very far from ours.

On hot days, like today, we like to do what we now call our go-go-chasing-waterfalls moments. We look up blogs and Instagram and old maps to track waterfalls in the surrounding bush and make plans to discover new ones, and maybe revisit an old favourite from last summer. We pack plums and nectarines and apricots. We pull on our swimmers and shorts and caps, and yell slip-slop-slap as we pile into the car, and whoever shotguns the front seat is DJ and plugs in our playlist requests, and we brace ourselves for the onslaught of summer traffic as everyone wants to exit this vast sprawling city and get out to the waterfalls that beckon beyond.

Icebergs. Fairlight. Mermaid Pools.

Still lying on the floor, we keep going with our list of ocean pools, and the prettier the name, the further we will drive later today, to where there are pools upon natural pools to lower our overheated bodies into, and we wonder aloud what it is that people in other cities do to make themselves feel better.

61

It is evening and my girlfriends slide off the rocks like seals into Gordons Bay. We are careful not to step down too hard. Last week Niki stepped on coral and for days she was digging out the splintered fragments with her French-polished nails.

Katie says, it's funny how each rock here seems to represent a different area of Sydney. On summer evenings this place is a regular scene.

There are the locals, she says, pointing to a group sprawled out on towels with mini speakers.

That's the city post-work set, and see, over there is Redfern and Marrickville, and we wave to some friends of friends we know who are tucked into a crevice, smoking. We watch as people pick their way across the rocks, trying to find their tribe.

Tessa has bought a new swimsuit. It is a black one-piece with patterns cut into the sides and it plunges down into a deep V. She is sprawled out on the rocks soaking in the sun, wearing Ray-Bans, and her blonde locks are tousled.

She is telling Katie how she wants to move home, as she misses family and friends, but she is not sure what she will do back here because the acting industry is so small. Sydney can feel a bit like a giant country town, you know, she says. She thinks maybe she will give it another year to really try and crack LA. But she is worried, as she has been saying this every year, and she wonders where the line is between hope and delusion.

I say that it would be nice to have her back here, but also that I can imagine her shining on some screen. I tell her that things are longer and less inclined and smaller to change than we think they will be and we need to give them time.

Katie tells us she has left the food kitchen that was making her sad and has decided to set up her own bakery. She eventually wants to get a van and sell her pastries and cakes along the road while travelling the country.

We slip into the ocean and are all treading water when Tessa shrieks suddenly, there's something in the water! We turn quickly.

This is a fishing bay with no nets and it is known for attracting reef sharks. And although the chances of being taken are less than being struck by lightning, it still grips the heart, and it is hard not to get dragged into the aquatic, mythic pull. It is hard not to see our flimsy legs kicking uselessly beneath us and to un-imagine that swift shadow of death upon us.

It is a tale as old as time, we have all been told, one of beast and primal fear. And somehow their very shady existence forces us to acknowledge that, despite all the trappings of modernity, technology, and progress, there are still some things we have no control over. We have chosen to enter their watery realm and there are no assurances about the dark shapes beneath us.

Some women won't go into the water on the first day of their periods, for fear the scent of blood will lure the creature out. Many of my friends refuse to swim past the breakers, certain that sharks are waiting beyond the crashing waves. Scientists try to number, tag, and understand their seasonal patterns, and call for a cautious approach against the media's sensationalism of the threat of shark attacks. Governments pour millions into shark mitigation and surveillance devices. Others protest against shark protection, wanting some kind of mediaeval culling. They expect the ocean to be without danger, a playground for their desires.

But, no matter our stance, sharks dart into the crevices of our minds and call out to us.

Every year the media pulls out one of the dark underwater shapes and splashes it across the front pages. Tales of surfers taken by a Great White Shark off the rugged Western Australian coastline. Or a near-miss moment, complete with images of a body scarred by the teeth marks. Within friendship and family circles there are stories at Christmas time of close calls at beach gatherings, but most of us have never witnessed the creatures for ourselves. Yet we still cling to our superstitions.

We wrestle in our own small ways with our personal, modern-day Leviathan. Our fugitive sea monster, who reminds us that things are always moving beneath the surface, and reminds me of some passages my dad taught me from the Bible. Like Job, who calls into question how we will deal with our inner fears:

Will he keep begging you for mercy? Will he speak to you with gentle words? Will he make an agreement with you for you to take him as your slave for life? Who dares open the doors of his mouth, ringed about with his fearsome teeth? Who has a claim against me that I must pay? Everything under heaven belongs to me. Nothing on earth is his equal—a creature without fear.

The dark shape hovers next to Tessa, beneath the waves, and suddenly pushes above the surface, revealing a black labrador paddling frantically towards us, his head upright and proud, as the waves spill over and push his progress back. Tessa screams, and we all laugh, relieved, and pull ourselves out of the water, dripping like the half-women half-seals from my father's stories, claiming our rock in our part of Sydney.

62

We're going to Bat Hill for Sami's farewell, Niki texts me. Sami, Bowerbird, Niki, and her friend who is visiting from New York and has a slight lisp, all decide to meet after work at the highest point in Moore Park.

The sky is still bright, and I wear the watermelon shorts I bought for five dollars at the second-hand shop.

We bring olives and guacamole and cherries and mango and three types of cheese, and Bowerbird bakes hash fudge, and we pull out cold beers and clink them across the rugs and scarves laid out under us.

We sit together atop the hill, and for a moment we are royalty staring down at our loyal subjects, the landmarks of the city: the Centrepoint Tower, the AMP Building, the Harbour Bridge, the waves of the Opera House—these belong to us, and they twinkle for us in the fading light.

The bats streak across the sunset. They are coming from the Botanical Gardens, where they sleep in the trees all day like furry hanging pods, waiting for the light to settle before they fill the Sydney skies.

I used to work late shifts in a bar and when I finished I would walk home along Oxford Street among the shouts and bass and the neon lights that drew out the other creatures of the night as the bats rubbed their leathery wings above us and shrieked at the moon.

The friend says Sydney is not what he expected, and Sami asks him in what way.

I don't know, he says, but it feels almost familiar. I keep stepping out thinking I will know where to go, but then all the streets have been rearranged in a different order, so it's having a trippy effect on my reality. I don't know what that's called, like some kind of cousin of deja vu.

Niki tells us that a painting of a bird she did was named runner-up in a small art competition she entered. She says the painting will now be used in a design for the packaging of some local soaps.

I mean, it's a tiny prize, and it's just soap, she says, and maybe that's a form of selling out. But it felt so good to make something that was just for me again and to have that recognised.

Bowerbird makes a whooping sound and almost crash-tackles her to the ground in a hug and says, small is big, small is everything, and Niki laughs and tells him he's high.

We sing along with Drake on the iPhone speakers. We lie down and pretend we know what we're talking about as we point to the Southern Cross, the Big Dipper, and the star of Venus, as we take it in turns to pee tipsily in the scrub.

The friend looks at the sky and laughs and says he recognises nothing. All our stars are upside down.

Next month, we will move out of this house. Friends will come to pick at the remains of our dismantled life. Couches, desks, egg beaters, and Tupperware containers: they are all for the taking. Bowerbird, Niki, and Sami; each will make their way onto the next chapter. Chapters filled with the promise of overseas adventures, sharing new rooms with partners, jobs that glisten with the hope of a new way of being.

The Indigenous protesters near our house will be pushed out of their camp a couple of months later, and this block of land too will house new stories and lives, for better or worse.

Years ago, a friend was hit by a car near a parking lot in the outer suburbs of Sydney. We had a memorial at this carpark, near a Woolworths shopping centre, as cars backed in and out around us. And his father spoke about what an unremarkable, everyday, common place this was to die. What a nothing slab of useless concrete, attached to a mall, that would now forever be imprinted as the place where everything was lost.

We don't always get to choose the places that become everything to us.

Each day, we are building up the layers of sediment in a city's memory for ourselves, our lovers, our friends, our parents, our children. Each intersection or new train line—or that block of apartments that used to be a shop that burnt down once upon a time on a summer afternoon—becomes a sentence in our lives. And that area that used to be the housing commission flats, which has now been converted into a bar or a middle-class terraced dream home, is just another occasion to say, remember when . . .

The language of a city is all around us if we choose to read it. Call it what you want: hauntings, ghosts, or memories, they are the same thing.

I think about all the secrets this land holds, about the way we ignore the past and build blindly on top of it, and how, one day, not today, I will become part of this earth, like my father, and my bones will form a part of this city.

I heard once that you start to feel a kinship for a place when you have lost a loved one in its soil, and so, ashes to ashes, I am bound to this sunburnt land.

Next month I will bundle my clothes together, scrub the fridge distractedly, and try to sort through all the stuff that we accumulate when we stay in one place for too long, and with no real idea of what the future will bring, I will gently close the door behind me.

But for now, in this brief moment, sitting on our Mount Olympus, Sami is not nervous about moving to Dubai, Bowerbird is no longer fearful for his sister, Niki is not worried about putting her life in perspective, I am not scared of the dark shapes that lie in this city, and the friend is wishing he lived here, with us, beneath the bats and our upside-down stars, on this windswept hill.

ACKNOWLEDGEMENTS

I am deeply grateful to my agent, Mary Krienke, and to my editors, Michael Reynolds and Alaina Gougoulis, for believing in this book and amplifying the voice with such expertise, grace, and kindness. Thank you also to Szilvia Molnar, Jane Watkins, Tatiana Radujkovic and the entire wonderful team at Europa Editions and Text Publishing.

The first tendrils of this novel took place in Mexico at the Under the Volcano program. I am forever thankful to Magda Bogin and the Tepoztlán writing family: Jonathan Levi, Rebecca Levi, Natalie Hart, Jennifer Clement, Dhyan Adler-Belendez, Alison Wearing, Khaldun Ahmad and The Dawsons for their hospitality. To Ayşegül Savaş for realising the core of this novel and feeding it with her intuition, books, and Parisian breakfasts.

Heartfelt thanks to those who have read my work at different stages and gave their guidance and wisdom: Jess Brewster, Azhar Ali, Emily Maguire, Stella Kirkby. For all the conversations and support thank you to Jess King, Jacob Fry, Peter Callender, Chris McGillion, Gemma Atkinson, Alex Parker, Laura Collie, Tom van Nuenen, Megan Bolton, Asher Galvin.

Thank you to the various grants, funding bodies, and writing programs for providing the space to nurture my own writing practice: Australia Council for the Arts, Churchill Fellowship, Westwords, Faber Writing Academy, BYDS (Outloud) team, Writing NSW.

To Sydney and to all the places that helped inform this novel. Some parts of the book were written in Tepoztlán, Barcelona, Chennai, London, Berlin, whilst other parts were written in my car, on the train, in various share houses, independent book stores and in my childhood home; all of which I am equally grateful for.

Thank you to my Nani, Thatha, and Grada for their unwavering support and blessings and to all my aunts and uncles and cousins and family who are in Australia and scattered across the globe. To my mother for her vast imagination and love. To my father for first guiding me towards loving literature, and for all of the poetry for all of the years we had.

For the healing traditions and light workers that have taught me how to deal with grief and to write from the body as well as the mind. And finally, to all those who know what it means to have lost so much, because they love so hard.

About the Author

Kavita Bedford is an Australian-Indian writer whose stories and essays have appeared in *Guernica* and *The Guardian*. She teaches media, anthropology, and yoga in Sydney. *Friends and Dark Shapes* is her debut novel. www.kavitabedford.com